Cry of the West
Finding Home Series

Hallie

Verna Clay

*Dedicated to those possessing the pioneer spirit of adventure
…even the tiniest bit.*

Cry of the West
Finding Home Series
Hallie

For information contact:
VernaClay@VernaClay.com
Website: www.VernaClay.com

Publisher
M.O.I. Publishing
"Mirrors of Imagination"

Cover Design
Verna Clay

Editor
Jami Carpenter (Redpen girl)

Picture
CanStock: zastavkin

Dear Readers,

Writing Hallie's story has been a labor of love. For a long time I contemplated writing a book encompassing the Oregon Trail, and the more research I did as the story unfolded, the more I fell in love with the pioneers who gave up everything to follow their dreams and the Native Americans adversely affected by westward migration. The hardships endured by both groups are unimaginable.

In writing this story, I am in no way attempting to typify the lives of those who braved the Oregon Trail or the Native Americans impacted. My story has been written solely as romantic entertainment, but with the added aspect of research.

Regarding historical accuracy, I attempted to remain true to history but fudged one event, which I shall explain shortly. As for the locations described in *Cry of the West,* I decided it would be helpful if fabricated locations were known prior to the reading of the story. Other than those listed below, the locations and information remain true to my research.

The Oregon Trail began in Missouri, not far from St. Louis, and crossed in greater or lesser degrees, the states we now know as Kansas, Nebraska, Wyoming, Idaho, and Oregon. For much of "trail" history, these states were considered territories. For the timeframe of my book — 1866 — Oregon and Kansas were already admitted as states of the Union.

I hope you enjoy your journey from Westport Landing in Missouri to the Willamette Valley in Oregon. Of course, any inaccuracies other than indicated below, are inadvertent and I take responsibility for them.

Fabrications from my imagination are: the steamship, *Mirabella;* the towns of Jebson and River Bend Grove; Muddy Creek Valley; and the Brandon Hotel.

The tornado that struck St. Louis in 1866 is factual; however, it happened in October, not March.

Enjoy the Adventure,

Verna Clay

Order of books in the *Finding Home Series:*

Hallie: Cry of the West
Lilah: Rescue on the Rio
Daisy: Missouri Challenge

Table of Contents

Prologue

Chapter 1: Finding Courage 1

Chapter 2: Unexpected Request 4

Chapter 3: First Names, Please 14

Chapter 4: Traveling Companions 21

Chapter 5: No Room at the Inn 26

Chapter 6: All Aboard! 30

Chapter 7: Slime 39

Chapter 8: Westport Bound 53

Chapter 9: Land Legs 56

Chapter 10: Gee Haw 65

Chapter 11: "Westward Ho!" 79

Chapter 12: Caress 94

Chapter 13: Crossing the Wakarusa 101

Chapter 14: Carvings at Alcove Spring 107

Chapter 15: Bad Dream at Fremont Springs 114

Chapter 16: Narrow Escape at The Narrows 118

Chapter 17: The Lone Tree 126

Chapter 18: Platte Incident 131

Chapter 19: Fancy Girlfriends 143

Chapter 20: Descending Windlass Hill 147

Chapter 21: Eyeful at Ash Hollow 156

Chapter 22: Release at Register Cliff 161

Chapter 23: Blessing 176

Chapter 24: Audaciousness 181

Chapter 25: Reconciliation at Independence Rock 185

Chapter 26: Parting of the Waters and Parting of the Ways 190

Chapter 27: Sad Times at Clover Creek 194

Chapter 28: Heart to Heart at Shoshone Falls 199

Chapter 29: Showdown at Fort Boise 208

Chapter 30: Goodbye Farewell Bend; Hello Blue Mountains 220

Chapter 31: Decisions…Again 226

Chapter 32: The Barlow Road: Conquer or Be Conquered 229

Chapter 33: Beginning Again at the End 233

Chapter 34: Sowing and Reaping 237

Chapter 35: Letter 239

Chapter 36: Not Just Another Day 241

Epilogue 243

Research Materials for *Hallie: Cry of the West* 245

Author's Note 247

Rescue on the Rio: Lilah (Finding Home Series) 249

Prologue

March, 1866

With one arm around her eight-year-old son, Hallie Wells swiped her eyes with the handkerchief clenched in her other hand, trying to remain stoic. When men from her church began lowering her husband's coffin into his freshly dug grave, she bit her lip until she tasted blood to keep from sobbing, wanting to wail when the first pitch of dirt sounded on the simple wooden box.

Timmy, who had been so brave the past two days, turned into her side and buried his face against her bosom, his thin body shaking with gut-wrenching sorrow. Hallie's heart broke for her child who had loved his father dearly.

The pastor's wife placed a hand on Hallie's shoulder as Pastor Murdock said kindly, "Hallie and Timmy, it's time to leave."

Still clutching her son, Hallie turned slowly from the grave, but at the last minute paused and stared at her husband's coffin. She whispered, "I'll fulfill our dream, Thomas, I promise," and then released the sob she had been trying so valiantly to keep inside.

Chapter 1: Finding Courage

The crackling fire usually so comforting on a cold night did little to dispel Hallie's anxiety. Staring into the flames, she took deep breaths and closed her eyes, but her mind refused any semblance of peace.

Tom, why did you have to be in the wrong place at the wrong time? Why did fate send you to St. Louis on the same day as a tornado?

In the week since Thomas's burial, Hallie and Timmy mourned his loss, though in different ways. Usually outgoing and rambunctious, Timmy became reserved and quiet, while Hallie, hoping to still her fears for a while, weeded flower beds and scrubbed and cleaned the cabin that had been her home with her husband and childhood sweetheart for the past seven years.

Now, with Timmy in bed and her head drooping from exhaustion—sorrow, laced with fear of the future for her son and herself—could no longer be held at bay, and her tears coursed unhindered. That awful day when Pastor Murdock galloped to her farm with the sad news of her husband's demise replayed itself in her mind. The kindly pastor had tried to offer some consolation by explaining that Thomas, shielding a little girl from debris thrown by the tornado and saving her life, was struck himself, and according to the deputy, most likely did not suffer since he never regained consciousness.

The thought of her sweet husband being so brave brought a fresh wave of tears, but for a few minutes

Hallie allowed herself the unreasonable feeling of anger toward Thomas for dying and leaving her and Timmy alone. Her anger was soon replaced with self-pity because now they had nothing, all their worldly belongings having been sold a month earlier in anticipation of their upcoming travel.

Finally, with her anger and sorrow spent, Hallie inhaled a shuddering breath, stared into the orange flames, and resolved to find a solution to her dilemma. Methodically, she inventoried her predicament—she had no home, no employment, and practically no belongings. What she did have, however, was the reason for Thomas's trip to St. Louis. In his pocket were three tickets for passage aboard the steamboat *Mirabella* leaving in mid April from St. Louis to Westport Landing. She also had enough money to purchase a wagon, oxen, and supplies necessary to continue from Westport with the train headed west on the Oregon Trail.

You have more than that; you have the dream Thomas inspired.

For the first time in days, Hallie smiled.

Tom, your dream of adventure and new beginnings was infectious.

For a few minutes, she envisioned the land her husband had diligently researched—the Willamette Valley in Oregon. Even now, his enthusiastic voice rang in her ears. "It's the next best thing to heaven, honey. So beautiful it steals your breath away. We'll start a new farm with crops that fairly burst from the ground they're so happy at being sown. We'll build a home to last through generations. We'll have the adventure of a lifetime. Can't you hear the Cry of the West? Come on, Hallie, say you'll consider it."

A log popped, hissed, and crumbled, the sound bringing Hallie back to the present and crumbling her memory of that magic moment—but not her reply, which was the same today as it had been on that glorious day—"Yes, I'll go!"

Shoring up her resolve to continue onward to Oregon, Hallie determined that her next step was to hire a man to drive the wagon she'd purchase in Westport. She would have to budget carefully in order to pay him and the expenses of their journey, as well as the beginnings of her new life in Oregon, but it was all doable.

Finally, she dozed in her rocking chair dreaming of beautiful Oregon, a new state full of opportunity in this vast United States.

Chapter 2: Unexpected Request

Cooper Jerome cursed and began walking the short distance from Jebson's Livery to Jebson's General Store so as to pass the time while his horse was being shod.

Dammit, Sweet Pea, why couldn't you wait until we got home to throw a shoe?

Cooper glanced at Vernon's Saloon and felt the pull of cheap whiskey. He wanted a drink—bad. So bad, in fact, his steps faltered and his courage wavered.

Bolstered with determination, he hastened his steps across the street and down the boardwalk to the store and saw Mrs. Wells enter with her son. He'd heard tell that her husband was killed in the tornado that hit St. Louis. He felt sorry for her, but she was young and would most likely find another husband—probably a widower with a few kids—and life would go on. She wasn't outright pretty, but she was passable.

He remembered meeting the Wells shortly after being discharged from the army and settling into the small farm he'd bought six months previous. Mr. Wells walked with a pronounced limp and a brace on one leg and Cooper wondered if he suffered from the ravages of infantile paralysis. As for Mrs. Wells, he'd never forgotten the color of her eyes—as green as the grass on Kentucky hills. One of the locals had introduced them outside of Jebson's store, the gathering place for local gossip and news. In fact, Toliver Jebson and a slew of brothers, sons, cousins, and other family members, owned just about everything in the small town of Jebson, twenty miles east of St. Louis.

After that first meeting, he'd transacted a couple of animal purchases with Mr. Wells when he bought a mule and some chickens to get his farm going.

Returning his thoughts to the present, Cooper knew the neighborly thing to do would be to offer his condolences. By the time he entered the store, however, Mrs. Wells had disappeared into the back room jammed with fabric bolts and sewing supplies. Rather than follow her into that part of the store, he decided to buy a case of shells for his twin Smith and Wesson six-shooters and wait for her to return.

* * *

Hallie pretended interest in a bolt of blue gingham while she tried to steady her rapid breathing.

"Ma, can I go see if Zack and Zeke are out back?" Timmy asked.

"Sure. Just don't get so caught up you don't hear me when I call."

"Okay, Ma."

Hallie breathed a sigh of relief. She didn't want Timmy overhearing her when she talked to Mr. Jerome. She'd seen the tall cowboy crossing the street toward the general store and then heard the door open when he entered. Her mind shouted, "Ask him!"

She'd met Mr. Jerome a couple of times before and later observed to Tom that he looked like a haunted man. Her husband had replied, "He's recently returned from the War of the States as a Union soldier and bought that ramshackle old Richardson place." He had sighed and continued, "That's what war does to a man, especially when its brother-against-brother." After that, Tom had pointed to his bum leg caused from a childhood bout with paralysis and said, "I guess something good did come of this. I didn't have to fight in a war and kill my fellow Americans."

Hallie heard Timmy call a greeting to Mrs. Jebson and then open and close the door as he went in search of his friends. Gathering her wits, she reentered the front of the store and bumped into Mr. Jerome when she rounded the door frame. Inadvertently, she gasped and placed a hand over her heart.

"Sorry, ma'am, I didn't mean to frighten you."

His voice was rich and deep and Hallie was suddenly tongue-tied. The man was so—she searched for a word—masculine: over six feet tall, with wavy black hair tied back with a leather strap and a face that seemed carved from granite with its angles and planes. Blue eyes that would make the loveliest shade for a dress stared at her above cheeks and jaws that hadn't seen a razor for days. She couldn't decide whether his looks favored that of an angel or a devil. Her courage almost failed, but then she remembered Tom saying that Mr. Jerome was a just and good man.

In a breathless voice, she said, "Hello, Mr. Jerome. You're just the man I wanted to see."

He gave her a questioning look. "Is that right?"

"Yes, sir. Do you suppose we could walk onto the porch? I'd like to discuss a proposition with you that is of a private nature."

Mr. Jerome quirked an eyebrow and Hallie turned scarlet when she realized the suggestive nature of her remark.

6

He stepped aside, motioning toward the door with his hand. "After you, ma'am."

Hallie prayed her heartbeat would slow down. If it didn't, she might faint.

Amidst curious glances from Mr. and Mrs. Jebson, they stepped out onto the boardwalk. She walked a few paces and then turned around, fisting her hands in her skirt. *Just ask him. All he can do is say no.*

Before she could speak, he said, "Mrs. Wells, I'd like to offer my condolences on the loss of your husband. He was a good man."

"Thank you, Mr. Jerome. Yes, he was a very good man. He also said that of you." She paused considering how to proceed. Mr. Jerome's blue eyes and intent stare unnerved her and muddled her thoughts. She grazed her teeth over her bottom lip.

"Ma'am, please say whatever it is that's troubling you."

It's now or never. "Um, I'm not sure if you heard that Thomas and I sold our farm and just about everything we own, including the animals. For years, he wanted to move west. It was a dream that eventually became my dream as well. We purchased a reservation with a wagon train headed out of Westport next month. The money we received from the sale of our property was for the purchase of a wagon, oxen, supplies, and also to hire hands to help with the building of our cabin on one hundred acres that Tom bought in the Willamette Valley in Oregon." She'd spoken the words in a rush and ended with, "The new homeowners are taking possession soon. They've been accommodating since Tom's death, but they sold their own place and need to move in."

Hallie watched Mr. Jerome furrowed his brow. After a long silence, he asked, hesitantly, "So, what is it you need from me?"

* * *

The expression on Mrs. Wells' face wasn't giving Cooper a good feeling. She wanted something and he definitely had the notion he wasn't going to like what it was, especially when she couldn't meet his eyes.

Unexpectedly, her emerald gaze stared directly at him and his gut clenched, and when the breeze blew a stray lock of her light brown hair across her forehead, he almost moved his hand to tuck it back under her bonnet.

"Mr. Jerome, would you be interested in driving my wagon to Oregon? I would pay you well."

Cooper blinked, forcing himself to look away from the pleading in her eyes. "Uh, well, ma'am…" He glanced back. She looked like she was about to cry. "Uh, ma'am, now that would take me away from my place through planting season and harvest, and longer." He dreaded her expression if he flat out refused.

"I would pay you whatever you would make during harvest and more." She blinked and brushed at a tear that kept welling up in one eye. "Mr. Jerome, I'm desperate. I have no home. I have no husband. I have no family to turn to. I have a young son to care for. And I have very little time to prepare before departure. The wagon train leaves the end of April. Believe me, if I were capable of driving the oxen myself, I would do so. But, as you can see, I am neither large, nor strong. I fear

I would kill myself and my child. Besides, I doubt the train master would even allow me near the team after he saw me crack a whip." She gave a pathetic smile at her attempt at a joke.

Cooper forced his eyes away from hers and glanced down the street at the big SALOON sign. He wanted that drink. Stalling for time, he removed his Stetson, slapped it against his thigh, replaced it, scratched his neck, and finally met her gaze again. "Give me some time to think about it."

Her joyous expression transformed her face from plain to pretty. *Dammit, Cooper. Just tell her no and walk away.*

* * *

After thanking and excusing herself from Mr. Jerome, Hallie went back inside the shop and finished making her purchases. Then she stepped to the outside wall of the general store to call down the narrow alley for Timmy.

"I'm comin', Ma."

While she waited for her son, she couldn't stop the surge of hope that kept trying to break free. Since Tom's death her emotions were in constant turmoil, worrying for the future of her son and herself. Life without a husband was not easy, especially if one were destitute of a home. Mr. Jerome said he'd ride out to her place in a couple of days with his answer.

Glancing down the street she saw him exit the livery and mount his horse. He was a big man and the thought of him driving the oxen and protecting her and Timmy on the five-month journey filled her heart with hope yet again.

Timmy rounded the corner of the building yelling goodbye to Mr. Jebson's sons and holding a lizard firmly, but gently, in his grasp. He looked up and smiled. "See what I found, Ma."

Hallie ruffled his blond hair, a shade lighter than his father's had been, and smiled.

Timmy eyed his mother. "Ma, you okay? You look kinda…happy, again."

"I'm feelin' better. How about you?"

Timmy sighed. "Yeah, I'm feelin' better, too." He paused. "But I sure miss Pa."

Hallie knelt and hugged him. "We're always going to miss him, son. But we have to go on."

Two days later, as promised, Mr. Jerome trotted his horse to the front of her cabin. The nervousness that had been giving Hallie stomach trouble for days now started her heart pounding furiously. What would she do if he said no?

* * *

Cooper glanced around the tidy yard surrounding Mrs. Wells' cabin. Beds of climbing roses twisted their vines up the posts and lattice of the porch, promising a burst of color and fragrance any day now. His gut twisted. He was going to tell her that he wouldn't be accompanying her on the Oregon Trail. Hell, it had only been a short time since his return from the nightmare of war and he'd dreamed of farming his own land for years.

Refusing to let his thoughts drift to the things he had seen and done in that God awful war, he turned his attention to the front door opening.

Mrs. Wells greeted him with a shy smile and his gut twisted some more. "Good afternoon, Mr. Jerome. Please come in and have some tea."

Cooper wanted to blurt a refusal of the tea, decline his assistance in driving her wagon, and gallop far away from her green eyes.

"Thank you, ma'am. That would be right nice."

He followed her inside. The cozy atmosphere fairly reeked with a woman's touch. She motioned to a large table in the center of the room.

"Please have a seat, Mr. Jerome. I also have oatmeal cookies just out of the oven. Do you like oatmeal cookies?"

Cooper saw her wring her hands together. She was as nervous as he was. "I like them very much."

She smiled, waited for him to sit, and then rushed to a sideboard, pouring a glass of tea and placing cookies on a plate. Bringing her offering to the table, she set it in front of him and then sat down across from him.

Cooper removed his hat and stowed it on the chair next to him. Mrs. Wells said, "Oh, where are my manners? Let me hang your hat on the hook by the door." She started to rise.

"Don't worry about it." He shot a hand out to stop her and immediately wanted to curse when he saw her eyes widen at his touch. He jerked his hand back and lifted a cookie. "Aren't you having one, too?"

Still flustered, she said, "Oh, not now. I always eat pinches of cookie dough while I'm baking. By the time they come out of the oven, I'm too full to eat any more."

She bit her full bottom lip, something Cooper decided was a habit when she was nervous, and he quickly glanced away. This was becoming more difficult by the second. He said, "Looks like we might get some rain this afternoon."

Mrs. Wells didn't respond and he glanced back at her. She wore a sad expression.

"You've come to decline my offer, haven't you, Mr. Jerome?"

Damnation! Don't look at me like that. "Uh, y…"

The door burst open and her boy ran in. "Howdy, Mr. Jerome. Are you takin' us to Oregon?" he asked loudly.

Cooper looked at the scrawny, tow-headed boy with a dirt-streaked face and cowlicks sending his hair in several directions, and his heart dropped to his feet. The boy reminded him of…

Mrs. Wells said, "Timmy, it's very rude to interrupt grownups by bursting into a room. As for Mr. Jerome accompanying us to Oregon, he said–"

Cooper interrupted. "I said, yes. I'll be driving your oxen and making sure you're settled in your new place." He glanced at Mrs. Wells' rounded eyes and wondered when he'd lost his mind.

Timmy shouted, "Yes! Thank you! Thank you!" He ran to his mother and hugged her. "Oregon—here we come!"

Cooper looked from the boy to his mother just as two big tears slid down her cheeks. Quickly, she swiped them with her apron and returned her son's hug. "Timmy, you go feed the chickens while Mr. Jerome and I discuss the particulars of the move."

"Sure, Ma." He looked at Cooper and grinned, showcasing a missing front tooth.

After the boy slammed through the door, Mrs. Wells asked, "Why did you change your mind? Was it Timmy?"

"Yes, ma'am. But it's not something I want to explain."

"Then I'll not ask you to."

An awkward silence filled the cabin.

"Um, ma'am, why don't you tell me everything you can about your scheduled departure time, so I can make some plans?"

Chapter 3: First Names, Please

Cooper nailed the final board in place covering the door of his humble cabin, hoping to deter thieves while he was gone. He'd already delivered his animals, all but Sweet Pea, to a neighbor's care.

Shaking his head, he wanted to berate himself for his spur-of-the-moment decision to help the Wells widow and her son, but with everything in him, he knew it was really the only choice he had. Life was harsh for a woman without a husband, especially a woman with a young son and no home. He sighed.

The poor woman couldn't be much older than twenty-seven or eight, if that, and with her farm already sold, she was in deep trouble if she didn't remarry. He'd seen plenty of destitute women trying to survive during the war. A few lucky ones got jobs as teachers, but even that didn't pay much. Hell, he didn't even know if Mrs. Wells had an education, although she'd seemed learned. Some women took in washing, which paid little and aged them almost overnight, while others finally turned to prostitution to put food in their children's mouths. Although unlikely, just the possibility of that poor woman forced into a life of degradation sickened him. And the boy, God help him, the boy reminded him of another boy. Yep, he'd done right by her and her son.

With a final sigh, he checked his saddle bags and mounted Sweet Pea.

* * *

Hallie twisted around in the buckboard to check on Timmy sitting next to Daisy Smithson, the only child of the new owners of her farm. The red-haired girl with a mischievous tilt to her chin whispered in her son's ear. Timmy jerked his head back and shouted, "No way!"

Hallie smiled at the antics of the children and turned back around. Watching Timmy momentarily gave her respite from the finality of leaving the home that she and Thomas had shared. As the buckboard pulled onto the road in front of the farm, however, she said a silent goodbye to her dear husband. *Goodbye, my love. I'm following our dream.*

Brushing a tear aside, she basked in the familiar terrain that she might never see again. Mr. Smithson seemed to realize her need for reflection and did not interrupt her musings.

After several minutes travel, Hallie broke the silence. "I'd like to thank you again for the ride to town and the kindness you and Mrs. Smithson have shown Timmy and me by allowing us to remain on the farm even after you'd moved in."

The sweet man, whose wife was just as sweet-natured, replied, "It's the least we could do considering your circumstances. If we hadn't already sold our own place, we could have canceled the transaction so you could stay on."

"Now, I don't want you to fret about that. This is what Thomas wanted, and he put that same vision in me. I just feel blessed to have Mr. Jerome driving our wagon. For awhile, I wasn't sure how things would work out, but the good Lord sent us a good man."

"I'm right happy to hear that, ma'am." Mr. Smithson shifted the reins to his other hand, guiding the horses around a pothole.

After almost an hour, they arrived on the outskirts of town. "Now where exactly are you meeting Mr. Jerome?" asked Mr. Smithson.

"He said he'd meet us in front of the Grand Hotel. We're traveling by stagecoach to St. Louis and then on to Westport Landing by steamboat." Hallie could barely contain her excitement. She glanced around at Timmy and he gave her a smile that warmed her heart.

Mr. Smithson pulled the buckboard to the main cross street in town and guided the horses to the hotel, sitting on a corner. Contrary to its name, the Grand Hotel wasn't so grand with its faded façade in desperate need of whitewash and repairs.

Hallie anxiously scanned the few men smoking and laughing on the wide porch and an older couple strolling the warped boardwalk. Glancing farther down the street she saw Mr. Jerome dismounting his mare. As if her presence were a magnet, he turned and looked directly at her. Hallie's heart hammered. She was entrusting her life, and the life of her son, to a man she'd met fewer times than the number of fingers on one hand.

Mr. Jerome tipped his hat and then wrapped the reins of his horse around the hitching post.

Mr. Smithson jumped off the buckboard and came around to help Hallie down. Timmy and Daisy scrambled off the wagon's bed and Hallie chuckled when the impish girl unexpectedly planted a kiss on Timmy's cheek.

"Cut it out!" he admonished and jumped backward.

Daisy only grinned. "Don't forget what I said."

Timmy rubbed his cheek and replied, "You can't know that."

"Yes, I can."

"Cannot."

"You just wait and see, Timmy Wells," Daisy huffed, and climbed onto the seat Hallie had vacated.

Distracted by the exchange between Daisy and her son, Hallie jumped when Mr. Jerome said, "Mornin', ma'am," and placed her hand over her heart.

"Sorry, ma'am. Seems I have this way of startling you."

"No. No. I'm just nervous about leaving a place I've lived for so many years." She paused and then remembered Mr. Smithson. "Goodness, where are my manners? Mr. Jerome, I'd like you to meet Mr. Smithson. He's the gentleman who purchased my farm and he and his family have been angels during this difficult time. And this is his daughter, Daisy."

Mr. Smithson stuck out his hand. "I'm pleased to me ya, Mr. Jerome."

Mr. Jerome offered his hand in a firm shake. "Likewise, sir." He nodded and smiled at Daisy, "And pleased to meet you, too, little lady." He turned his attention to Timmy. "Good to see you again, Tim."

Daisy responded, "Howdy, sir."

Timmy responded, "You, too, Mr. Jerome."

He glanced at the back of the wagon. "I take it that's your trunk, Mrs. Wells."

"Yes. It contains all my worldly possessions," Hallie laughed nervously.

Mr. Jerome reached and tugged the trunk to the edge of the wagon bed. Mr. Smithson grabbed the handle on the other end.

In a flash, the trunk was safely stowed at the edge of the boardwalk to be reloaded when the stagecoach arrived. Hallie opened her reticule to peer at her pocket watch—ten thirty. The stage was due to arrive at twelve and leave at one with fresh horses for the four to five hour journey to St. Louis. She sure hoped it was on time.

Hallie glanced at her son, who was casting sour looks at Daisy. *What is wrong with Timmy's attitude?* She scowled and motioned for him to stand beside her.

Mr. Smithson reached to pat Timmy's shoulder. "Well, Timmy and Mrs. Wells, I guess this is goodbye. I wish you all the best in your new life and I'm right sorry about your husband."

"Thank you, Mr. Smithson. Again, I appreciate all you and your wife have done for Timmy and me."

Mr. Smithson smiled. "Well, you know our address, so don't forget to write. My Sarah loves gettin' letters."

Daisy smirked. "Yeah, Timmy, don't forget to write. Cause if you don't, someday I'll find you." She grinned, revealing a missing tooth just like Timmy's.

Timmy grumbled and gave her another sour look. Hallie chided, "Son! Mind your manners and tell Daisy goodbye."

He gave his mother a rebellious look, something unusual for him, and mumbled, "Bye, Daisy."

Hallie shook her head and was about to chastise him again when Mr. Jerome touched her elbow.

"Ma'am, you and Tim best wait on the porch while I check to see if any wires have been received about stagecoach delays.

The touch of Mr. Jerome's hand sent Hallie's heart racing. "Yes, of course." She stepped away from him and turned her attention toward her son. "Timmy, change your attitude and come with me." She grasped his hand and pulled him toward the porch as Mr. Smithson called a final farewell, commanded the horses, and flicked the reins. The buckboard pulled into the dusty road and Daisy waved goodbye to Timmy, blowing him a kiss.

Her son made a disgusted noise and turned his back toward the street.

Mr. Jerome motioned to two chairs on the hotel portico. "Why don't ya'll have a seat and I'll be right back? Can I bring you some tea or lemonade before I take care of business?"

Timmy appeared to have reverted back to his congenial self and waited for his mother to respond. Knowing that lemonade was one of her son's favorite drinks, she said, "Thank you, Mr. Jerome. Lemonade would be much appreciated."

Mr. Jerome started to turn away, but paused. "Ma'am?"

"Yes, Mr. Jerome?"

"Do you 'spose we could do away with the formalities since we're going to be traveling together for the next few months? Please call me Cooper. May I call you Hallie?"

Hallie felt her face flush scarlet and stumbled over her reply. "Oh…yes…that…that would probably be best, Mr. Jerome." His lips quirked and Hallie felt her face flame brighter. "I...I mean...Cooper."

Cooper's half grin turned into a full one. "Well, 'scuse me, Hallie and Tim; I'll be right back with your lemonades."

Chapter 4: Traveling Companions

The stagecoach departed only two hours past its scheduled time. Cooper shrugged and said he'd waited for as long as two days for a coach to arrive. Now, over an hour into their journey, Hallie's excitement mellowed and she felt her eyelids droop; sleepless nights had caught up with her.

Timmy, after discussing the Wild West with the only other child on the coach, a younger boy, around five, who couldn't stop fidgeting, now leaned against his mother's shoulder and succumbed to sleep. And the boy who'd asked his parents every few minutes, "Are we almost to St. Louey?" yawned, crawled onto his father's lap, and also fell asleep, his soft snores filling the coach.

Meeting the child's parents, Mr. and Mrs. Hankerson, a couple from a neighboring town and bound for the same wagon train as Hallie, was an unexpected bonus; they turned out to be delightful people.

Hallie yawned and glanced out the stagecoach window at Cooper riding alongside on his beautiful mare. Before her eyes closed, an unguarded thought escaped. *What a magnificent man on a magnificent horse.* She sighed and felt safe for the first time in weeks.

The slowing of the coach awakened Hallie and she realized she must have slept for quite some time because the sun was much lower on the horizon. Sammy, Timmy's newfound friend, had moved from his father's lap to sit beside Timmy, and the boys thumbed through a book about the Wild West, mesmerized by drawings of cowboys, Indians, horses, herds of buffalo, mountains, and other scenes the artist had encountered during his own journey west.

She glanced at Mrs. Hankerson, a pretty, full-figured, dark-haired woman, who said, "I was wondering when we'd take a break. I feel like every bone in my body has jarred loose."

Hallie nodded her agreement and stretched her aching neck. The stagecoach came to a complete halt and Cooper opened her door. "Let me assist you out."

While Mr. Hankerson helped his wife and son out the other door, Hallie accepted Cooper's extended hand. It felt warm and calloused and sent a frisson of awareness up her arm. As soon as her feet touched the ground, she quickly withdrew her hand and stepped aside. Timmy jumped down behind her. The Hankersons rounded the coach and Mr. Hankerson turned to his son. "Sammy, I think we'd best head off into the bushes and take care of business." He looked at Hallie, "Would you like me to take Timmy with us?"

Hallie looked at Timmy. "Do you need to relieve yourself, son?"

"Yes, Ma."

"Okay, go with Mr. Hankerson."

After the boys left, Mrs. Hankerson sidled up to Hallie and whispered in her ear. "I don't know about you, but I think I'm going to wet my knickers."

Hallie looked at her sympathetically. "I know exactly what you mean," she whispered back. She glanced at Cooper to see him watching them and felt her face glow pink.

He cleared his throat and pointed. "Uh, ladies, see that tree over yonder? If you'd like to visit it, I'll make sure no one walks in that direction. And here, I have a blanket you can hold up for privacy." He took the couple of steps to his horse and untied a roll fastened to the back of his saddle.

Cooper's consideration of the needs of her bladder made Hallie want to throw her arms around him in gratefulness. *Throw your arms around Cooper! Hallie Wells, what's gotten into you? You watch the direction of your thoughts!*

After everyone had regrouped, the driver yelled, "All aboard! We'll reach St. Louis just after nightfall."

Relieved that the bumpy journey was almost over, Hallie settled back inside the coach and thought about the next leg of her adventure. Timmy must have been thinking the same thing, because he said, "Ma, I can't wait to ride on the steamboat!" Sammy caught his enthusiasm and agreed. "Oh, yeah! Let's see if we can find a picture of a boat in the book."

Hallie smiled and smoothed Timmy's tousled hair. He huddled next to his new friend and poured over their book again. Hallie glanced across at Mr. and Mrs. Hankerson. "I'm so happy we're traveling on the same wagon train and steamboat. And please, you must call me Hallie."

Mrs. Hankerson reached to pat her husband's hand. "And you must call us by our first names, as well— Lydia and Emmett."

"Have either of you been on a steamboat before?" Hallie asked.

Lydia replied, "I haven't, but Emmett has." She giggled. "Before he met me, he was a little wild."

Glancing back at the short, thin man, probably in his mid thirties, with rosy cheeks and an already receding hairline, Hallie found that impossible to believe.

Emmett smiled and admitted, "As a young pup, while sowing my wild oats, so to speak, I had a fondness for the cards and found myself gambling on riverboats often." He laughed. "But I was never very good at bluffing. After losing my hard-earned ranch wages one time too many, it cured me of the seamy side of life."

"Goodness, do you suppose they'll have card games and a saloon aboard our steamboat?" Hallie asked with incredulity.

"It's a possibility, but we'll just avoid that part of the boat. Besides, you said Mr. Jerome is escorting you. He's a formidable looking cowboy so no one will bother you. Even in my wild days I wouldn't have wanted to tangle with him."

Hallie glanced at Lydia. She could read the question in the woman's eyes about her relationship with Cooper, and she felt embarrassed. It was highly unorthodox for a woman to travel in the company of a man who wasn't her husband. Hallie had been so concerned about finding someone to drive her oxen that she hadn't even considered the speculations that would surely occur.

Not wanting to bring up the topic of her husband's death in front of Timmy, when he seemed so happy at the moment, she made a mental note to later clarify her strictly business relationship with Cooper Jerome for her newfound friends.

Chapter 5: No Room at the Inn

After dusk, the stagecoach unloaded its passengers at the Brandon Hotel in St. Louis. The weather had turned chilly and Hallie pulled her wrap tightly around her. Buttoning Timmy's jacket, she supposed they would spend the night at the hotel; that is, if accommodations were available. She sighed. There was so much about her journey that depended on circumstances at any given moment. Her ordered life no longer existed. Mentally and physically she squared her shoulders, hoping the action would strengthen her resolve. Being a timid woman, she had allowed Thomas to structure their lives. Of course, with his physical limitation, she had done her best to relieve the load of running their farm, but that in no way prepared her for the unforeseen happenings that were now part and parcel of her daily existence.

The opening of the stagecoach door interrupted her reverie and once again she grasped Cooper's extended hand so he could help her down. Timmy hopped the short distance to the ground, his eyes wide with curiosity. Emmett opened the other door and assisted Lydia and Sammy. Hallie heard the drivers yelling instructions and within a short time her trunk, as well as the Hankersons' trunk, was lowered to the ground.

Cooper suggested, "Hallie, why don't you and Tim wait in the portico while I see if I can secure a room and find bellboys to haul your trunk."

Hallie nodded and reached for Timmy's hand, drawing him up the steps and to a corner of the immense enclosed porch. This hotel seemed huge in comparison to the one in Jebson and Timmy's eyes rounded as he watched the comings and goings of cowboys with low slung, holstered revolvers, sophisticated women on the arms of business type men, and even women with rouged cheeks and fancy hats, enter and exit the hotel. Hallie felt overwhelmed herself.

Holding tightly to her son's hand, Lydia was guided by her husband to stand beside Hallie. She leaned toward Hallie and whispered loudly, "This shore ain't my little town of River Bend Grove."

Hallie smiled at her new friend. "And it's not Jebson either."

The women giggled and Emmett laughed along with them. He teased, "Lydia, I'll be right back. Don't start any trouble while I'm gone." He ruffled his son's hair and winked at his wife.

Hallie watched him enter the hotel and laughed nervously. "What if there aren't any rooms? Do you suppose we'll have to sleep in the stable?" She was only half kidding, but when she saw the startled look on Lydia's face, wished she'd kept her remark to herself.

* * *

Cooper stared at the hotel clerk and refused to back down. "Surely, there's got to be *something* available."

"Sir, as I've explained, this is the season for travelers making their way to the westward trails and we're *always* full up."

Cooper pushed his Stetson back and rubbed his forehead. He already had a headache and this yokel was making it worse. He glanced sideways and saw Mr. Hankerson enter the hotel. Sighing, he reached into his pocket and pushed a shiny coin toward the clerk. "Will this find us a room?"

The clerk slipped his hand over the coin and smiled, "Yes, I believe it will."

Cooper slipped another coin his way. "And how about this one for the man who just entered?"

The odious little man, who'd attempted to hide the bald spot directly on top of his head by slicking wiry gray hair over it, quirked a sidewinder grin at his double fortune, and surreptitiously palmed the coin off the counter.

Cooper motioned Mr. Hankerson over. "I was just informed that there are only two rooms left. How's that for luck?" As he watched relief wash over his traveling companion's face, he knew his coin had been well spent.

"That's terrific. I didn't want to return to my wife and son and tell them we'd be sleeping in the alley," he joked.

After they paid for their rooms and secured their keys, Mr. Hankerson turned to Cooper. "Please call me Emmett. May I call you Cooper?"

"Not a problem." Bouncing Hallie's key in his hand, he added, "Guess I'll give this to Mrs. Wells and then head on over to the stable to spend the night with my horse." *There, that should keep this guy from getting the wrong impression.*

Emmett made a waving motion. "Lead the way back to the ladies, sir."

The relief on Hallie's face when Cooper handed her the key made him feel like a hero. He said, "I'll see you and Tim in the morning—say, about eight. By that time, I'll have a buckboard hired to drive us to the dock." He glanced at Emmett. "Would you like to ride with us? There'll be plenty of room for everyone and the trunks."

"That's very kind, Cooper. And please, let me pay for the buckboard."

"That's not necessary."

Emmett laughed and repeated Cooper's earlier words, "The last two rooms in the hotel, huh? That was fortuitous timing, wouldn't you say? No, I'll reimburse you for the buckboard. We'll meet you out front at eight."

Cooper realized the ladies and children were glancing between the two of them with questioning looks. He turned to Hallie. "Well, ma'am, I'll see you in the morning."

He started to turn away, but her small hand on his elbow stopped him. With pretty pink cheeks, she asked, "Where will you be staying the night, Cooper?"

He grinned, "With my horse, ma'am. Sweet Pea gets right lonely when I'm not around." He laughed and descended the porch steps.

Chapter 6: All Aboard!

As planned, Hallie and Timmy were waiting at the front of the hotel at eight the next morning. So far, they hadn't seen the Hankersons.

The night before, Hallie had ordered dinner from the hotel dining room sent to their room. She knew Timmy had to be famished, as was she, and they relished a meal of beef stew with chunks of potatoes and carrots poured over a bed of rice, with large squares of cornbread, and for dessert, apple pie. Having saved back some of the cornbread she now unwrapped it and handed it to Timmy.

"Here, son; eat this until we can get a decent meal."

"Ma, I think you should have it. You didn't eat as much as me last night."

Timmy's thoughtfulness touched her heart; he had his father's same kindness. Longing for her dead husband clutched Hallie's emotions and caused her to blink rapidly to stop tears from falling. "No, honey, I want you to have it."

Timmy accepted the square but broke it in half. "Ma, you eat half. Okay? I wouldn't feel right eating it all myself." He handed her his offering. Hallie ruffled his hair and quickly ate her meager breakfast.

While they waited for Cooper she asked, "Son, I've been meaning to ask you about your attitude yesterday with Daisy. What was that all about? You two seemed to be friends up until then."

Timmy blushed and turned his head. "Aw, Ma, she said…she said we was gonna get married someday."

"What? Why would she think that?"

Timmy shuffled his feet. "She told me she had a dream 'bout it and it was so real she knew it was true."

Hallie stifled a smile. "Well, I'm glad you told me. Now I understand your attitude." Glancing up, she noticed Cooper heading toward them. She pointed, changing the subject. "Look, there's Mr. Jerome."

Timmy appeared relieved to drop the subject of Daisy's dream and waved at Cooper as he pulled the buckboard into the closest opening. Hallie waved also and wondered if Cooper had eaten. She felt guilty for not saving more cornbread. Perhaps they would have time to eat in the hotel dining room.

Hallie heard her name being called from the porch and turned around.

Lydia waved and called again, "Hallie, hello!"

Holding his father's hand, Sammy jumped up and down with excitement and shouted, "Hey, Timmy, we're gettin' on a boat today!"

Emmett grinned at his son, lifted him onto his shoulders, grasped his wife's elbow, and led her in Hallie's direction. Cooper reached her first, carrying a large sack. Wonderful smells wafted from the bag and Hallie's stomach growled.

He handed the sack to her and smiled. "Sure hope ya'll are hungry. I found a little diner and had the cook bag some breakfast. There should be enough for the Hankersons, too."

Timmy grinned. "Oh, yeah! Thank you, Mr. Jerome."

Hallie also thanked him and accepted the paper bag. When her hand brushed Cooper's, tingling shot up her arm. She opened the bag, feigning interest so he couldn't see the affect his touch had had on her.

Hallie, what's the matter with you? You should be ashamed of yourself.

The Hankersons stepped next to her and while Emmett and Cooper convened, she reached into the sack and began handing out huge fluffy biscuits, thick slices of bacon, and boiled eggs to the children.

Timmy and Sammy gobbled their food while the men loaded the trunks again. Soon, the buckboard was ready for departure.

The adults ate the remaining food until their expressions evidenced full bellies. Cooper said playfully, "I believe Oregon is calling our names. Shall we answer the call?"

* * *

Cooper lifted Hallie into the bed of the wagon and then Emmett lifted his wife and Sammy. In an exaggerated gesture, Cooper swung Timmy up beside his mother and the boy laughed freely, the sound bringing remembrances of his own son's laughter. He swallowed the lump in his throat and glanced at Hallie to see her watching him pensively.

Suppressing painful memories, he unhitched the horses and swung into the driver's seat beside Emmett. "We're about two miles from the wharf. After I drop ya'll off, I'll return the wagon to the stable and retrieve Sweet Pea."

Emmett nodded. "We sure appreciate your hospitality in allowing us to ride with you."

"The way I figure it, we'll be on this journey for a long time, and it won't be an easy one. I've traveled quite a bit in my life and the best way to get from one place to another is with folks watchin' each other's backs. There are some mean hombres in this world."

"You got that right. When I was a reckless young man, I almost got myself killed more than once. If Lydia hadn't come along and changed my wicked ways, I'd probably be dead by now."

Cooper chuckled, but didn't comment. Emmett, a short, thin man who looked more like an accountant than a farmer, seemed the least likely to be reckless. Of course, looks could be deceiving. Some of the meanest men Cooper had occasioned across during his own reckless days hadn't looked mean at all, and some of the meanest looking had been upstanding and righteous.

Cooper turned his attention back to the mules pulling their buckboard. The hard-packed road, already teaming with travelers in every mode of transport and pedestrians crisscrossing from one side to the other, required all of his attention. What with this being the traveling season for folks headed west, St. Louis was filled to overflowing. He sure hoped prices for supplies and a wagon wouldn't be sky high in Westport. Although Hallie had a hefty sum from the sale of her property, her money wouldn't go far if she wasn't prudent.

* * *

With Timmy sitting next to Hallie on their trunk and Lydia and Sammy across from her on their own trunk, they all stared wide-eyed at the bustling city. The pungent odors of fish and murky river hailed the approach of the dock even before Cooper turned the corner bringing their destination into view.

Timmy stood and cried, "Look, Ma! Is that our boat?"

In bold writing the word *Mirabella* was painted across the paddlebox and across the pilot house. "It sure is," Hallie exclaimed. "Timmy, sit down before you fall off the wagon."

Timmy and Sammy fidgeted excitedly as Cooper pulled the buckboard to the first open space and jumped off the wagon. "You ladies and boys wait here while Emmett and I check out the situation; see how they want us to load up."

Hallie patted her reticule. "Would you like our tickets now?"

"No, keep them until I get more information."

Hallie watched Cooper and Emmett walk toward the dock and offered a silent prayer of thankfulness that Cooper had agreed to help her. If she'd been forced to find her own way to Westport, the congestion and confusion of St. Louis would have been simply overwhelming. She'd only been to the city a handful of times in her entire life.

Born and raised south of St. Louis in an area known as Muddy Creek Valley, at the age of eighteen she'd married twenty-year-old Thomas and they'd lived with her parents while saving to buy their own place. Timmy was born in Muddy Creek Valley just a few years later. The sudden deaths of her parents in an influenza epidemic shortly thereafter had forced her and her younger sister to sell their childhood home to pay their parents' creditors. The remaining money was split between the women, with Lilah promptly leaving for New Orleans, and Hallie and Thomas purchasing their farm in Jebson.

Though Hallie and Thomas had urged Lilah to come live with them, she'd refused, insisting she was old enough to care for herself. After her move, she'd sent a letter praising New Orleans. Hallie wrote regularly, but Lilah only responded occasionally with short notes. That's how things had been for the past eight years. It had been six months since Lilah's last correspondence, which was an added worry for Hallie. Before leaving Jebson, Hallie had written her sister of Thomas's death and her intent to continue onward to Oregon.

Thinking about Lilah brought remembrances of Thomas. After the death of his widowed mother when he was seven, the childless aunt and uncle who'd raised him saw him and his disability as a burden. So it was no wonder he was more than happy to leave unhappy memories in Muddy Creek Valley. Always a dreamer, he'd fed his imagination by reading books packed with adventure and stories about the exciting territories to the west.

Brimming tears threatened to overflow and Hallie quickly returned her attention to the present to study the steamboat that would deliver them to Westport Landing. Remembering the information in the book Thomas had acquired about steamboats, she wasn't altogether ignorant. She knew the *Mirabella* was a side paddle wheeler because of its two paddles, one on either side of the hull. As with most steamships, there were three decks, the lowest being the main deck, the center, the boiler deck, even though boilers were not located on it, and the top, the hurricane deck. Atop the hurricane deck sat the pilothouse where the pilot, the most esteemed personage on a steamboat because of his knowledge of the river, with its many pitfalls of raging currents and snags, guided the ship from port to port. The best views were from the hurricane deck.

Surrounding the boiler deck, with its staterooms and centrally located dining room, was the promenade enclosed by gingerbread railings, a popular place for travelers to watch the river, converse, or stretch their legs by walking around the deck.

The main deck was for cargo, animals, and passengers unable to pay for staterooms.

Little Sammy's excited shout startled Hallie. "There's Pa!"

Hallie followed the direction he pointed and saw Cooper and Emmett walking back toward their buckboard. Anticipation gave her goose bumps. She moved her mouth in whispered words to her dead husband, "We'll soon be aboard the *Mirabella,* Tom."

* * *

Cooper's questions had gotten him instructions for boarding passengers and trunks, as well as Sweet Pea. His request that the Wells and the Hankersons have staterooms next to each other was met with a grunt from the mate and an unfriendly, "What'd'ya think this ship is, the *Great Eastern?* We gots so many pioneers headed for Westport, we'll be lucky ta get 'em all onboard."

Cooper glowered until finally the short, pudgy, greasy, salt-and-pepper-haired, smelly man said, "I ain't promisin' nothin', but tell the steward when ya board that Schmitty said ta give ya two rooms ta-gather. If'n he can, he will. That's the best I can do."

After thanking the man and heading back to the buckboard, Emmett said, "You know, Cooper, you got a scowl that would scare the stripes off a tiger."

Cooper glanced at the farmer, who today looked like a librarian or a teacher. "I guess I can thank hard livin' and the war for that."

Emmett said, "I wasn't in the war for reasons I'll keep personal, but I heard enough descriptions of battles to give me nightmares for days."

Cooper didn't respond. The last thing he wanted to do was reminisce about the war. His scowl softened when he saw Timmy's big grin and Sammy jumping up and down pointing at them. He almost laughed at Hallie biting her nails like a schoolgirl.

After moving the buckboard to the dock and unloading the trunks, Emmett waited with the women and children while Cooper returned the wagon to the stable and retrieved Sweet Pea. Within thirty minutes he was back at the dock hitching his horse to a post and rejoining them. After a lengthy wait in line at the landing stages, Hallie handed her tickets to a stocky young steward holding a clipboard. When Cooper informed him of Schmitty's approval for adjoining rooms, he grumbled, flipped through his roster, and wrinkled his brow. "I guess I can give you the Tennessee and the Texas rooms on the port side."

Cooper said, "Sounds good," and turned to Hallie and Emmet. "I'll get some roustabouts to deliver your trunks to your rooms and after I settle Sweet Pea on the main deck, I'll come find you."

* * *

Hallie held Timmy's hand and followed Emmett to their staterooms. The steamboat certainly wasn't one of the expensive ships that plied the Mississippi and Missouri Rivers with wealthy passengers. As Thomas had explained, it was a retired mid-class passenger steamer now transporting pioneers, cargo, and animals.

Emmett pointed to a grimy door with the word "Texas," painted across it. The door next to it was painted with "Tennessee." Opening the "Texas" door, Hallie stepped into a tiny room reeking of tobacco. A narrow bed was bolted to the far wall with another bed, bunk board style, above it. A tiny chest with two drawers and a lamp sitting in a holder fastened to the wall were the only other objects in the room, except for the key to the room resting on top of the chest. It was one of the dreariest rooms Hallie had ever seen.

While untying her bonnet ribbons, it suddenly occurred to her that her ticket was for one room shared by three people. Where was Cooper going to sleep?

Chapter 7: Slime

The *Mirabella* was finally loaded and readied for departure on the Missouri River in the early afternoon. Standing at the railing of the promenade on the boiler deck, Hallie watched Cooper's approach.

Looking plumb tuckered out, he said, "Guess ya'll had a bird's eye view of us trying to calm that spooked horse."

Hallie nodded. "That was friendly of you to help. Too bad the horse had to be led off ship. I thought he was going to charge into the drink a couple of times."

Timmy asked, "What's going to happen to him?"

Cooper shrugged. "His owner said he'll catch the boat again when it returns in ten days and put blinders on the horse."

Emmett glanced at his pocket watch, "Even after all that, we're only a couple of hours off schedule. Considering the trouble with that horse, that's pretty good."

From their vantage point, they observed roustabouts, mates, and stewards, under the watchful eye of the captain, hasten the ship for departure. In a short time, the whistle shrilled, the stacks puffed black smoke, and the paddles eased the ship into murky waters. Hallie squeezed Tim's hand. His voice held a sense of wonder. "Ma, we did it. Pa would be right proud."

Hallie felt so choked up, she couldn't respond.

After the *Mirabella* was well under way, a goodly portion of the crowd of passengers on the promenade drifted back to their rooms or found amusements elsewhere. Emmett and Lydia excused themselves and returned to their stateroom with Sammy.

Hallie said, "Timmy, run on to our room. I'll be there in a minute. I just need to discuss something with Mr. Jerome first." After Timmy left, she asked, "Where are you sleeping?"

"I'm on the main deck, bedding down outside Sweet Pea's stall."

Hallie frowned. "Please let me see if I can buy you a stateroom."

Cooper grinned, "No, ma'am. Sweet Pea and I have often been bed partners. Like I said before, she gets kinda lonely without me."

Although Cooper had been speaking of his horse, Hallie felt color rise to her face.

Chuckling again, his eyes captured hers and twinkled with a hint of amusement, "Don't worry about me, Hallie."

Now, hours later, after eating a supper of roast beef and potatoes with the Hankersons in the dining room on the same deck as their staterooms, Hallie lay on her narrow, lumpy bed, wondering what Cooper had eaten. She was disappointed when he didn't join them, and made a mental note to be sure he knew his meals were inclusive in the price of their tickets.

Trying to take her mind off her suffocating quarters, she thought about the view from the hurricane deck that she and Timmy had discovered with Emmett, Lydia, and Sam. Before supper, they had all gone to explore the ship, climbing the stairs to the top deck to enjoy the unobstructed views. The steamboat had moved into deep water and away from civilization and the scenery was simply breathtaking. Now, remembering the wonderful sights, Hallie wanted to escape her stuffy room and stargaze. How beautiful the stars would be on such a clear night. And maybe a little exercise would help her sleep when she returned. *No one will know.*

Hallie quickly lit her lamp and dimmed it, allowing just enough light to slip on the dress she had worn that day. Dealing with her corset wasn't something she relished, so she just pulled it over her nightgown; besides, who would see her in the dark if she kept to the shadows. Fastening the front buttons, she wished she could be this lax with her clothing all the time. On the farm, she hadn't worn a corset, but now, traveling and being around so many people, she didn't feel properly clothed without it.

Grabbing her cloak and donning her bonnet, she tied the ribbons under her chin and then as quietly as she could, pulled on her high top walking shoes, foregoing her stockings. With a glance at Timmy to make sure he was sleeping soundly, she smiled at his quiet snores and then slipped out the door, locking it.

The promenade was empty and she wished she'd looked at her watch. She decided it had to be after midnight since she'd lain in bed unable to sleep for hours.

Making her way to the stairs leading to the hurricane deck, she glanced over the railing enclosing the promenade and into the murky depths of black water glinting here and there under a full moon. Anxious to reach her destination, she almost tripped in her haste. *Maybe this wasn't such a good idea. Maybe I should just go back to my room. No! I'm almost there.*

With renewed determination, Hallie carefully ascended the stairs. Just as she had known, the stars were bright and big and beckoning. Her breath caught and she twirled in a circle, never taking her eyes off their teasing twinkles. *Oh, this was so worth it.*

Walking to the railing on the starboard side, she sighed with relief that the deck was empty. Soon she was marveling at the beautiful sky staring back at her— so far away, and yet she felt as if she could reach and capture a star. Finding the brightest one, she made a wish. *Starlight, starbright, I make a wish tonight. I wish for a safe journey and a bright new future. I wish...*

She paused to consider her next wish, *I wish for Cooper Jerome to find happiness because of his kindness to Timmy and me.*

She paused again to think if she had another wish. *I wish...*

Distant sounds distracted her. She heard what sounded like a slamming door and then muffled voices. For a second, she wondered if she should flee, but the voices stopped and she didn't see anyone. Besides, she was a long way from the card room in the aft of the ship and standing in the shadows, surely no one would see her. Dismissing her fears, she returned to stargazing and dreaming of the future.

Instead of allowing her mind to worry about the daunting task of acquiring a wagon, oxen, and supplies, she envisioned it already done, with Timmy and herself walking behind Cooper, who was walking beside the oxen, cracking his whip overhead and guiding the team down dusty trails. So engrossed was she in her daydream, she jumped when she heard a slurred, "Well, howdy, li'l lady. Ain't you a nice surprise?"

Hallie inhaled sharply and lifted her hand to her throat. Another voice said, "Ain't this our lucky night, Stubby."

"Shore is. My four aces put jingle in my pocket and yer full house did you good, too. Now, we gots a woman's comp'ny. What more could a man ask fer?"

Slowly, Hallie edged away. The men were blocking her exit, not moving. She decided to run toward the pilot house if they came closer.

"My husband just stepped away for an instant. He…he'll be right back." Her words sounded like the lie they were.

For a man so inebriated, Stubby moved fast, and before Hallie could run, he stepped to block any escape. A shaft of moonlight revealed his slimy appearance and grease matted hair and she almost fainted when she got a whiff of his foul breath. In a matter of seconds, the man named Harley snaked behind her and thrust an arm around her waist, trapping her arms and pulling her into the folds of his rotund body. When she opened her mouth to scream, a fat, stinky hand clamped over it.

Oh, God. Oh, God. Somebody help me. Cooper!

Stubby laughed softly and stuck his face in hers. "Either you ain't half bad lookin' or I'm too drunk to care." He snickered to his friend, "I'm gonna give her a feel, Harley; see if she's worth our time."

Hallie whimpered behind Harley's big hand and tried to bite it as Stubby reached to fondle her breast. Harley said, "Oh, she's gonna be worth it, Stubby. She just tried to bite my hand. She's got sass."

Stubby added, "She's kinda skinny, but all woman, that's fer sure. We's gonna have us a good ol' time tonight."

Out of nowhere, a deep-timbered voice calmly spoke, "I highly doubt that. Let her go, step away, and maybe I'll let you live." The click of a gun cocking, and then another, sounded as Cooper Jerome stepped into view. Aiming one pistol at Stubby and the second at Harley, he looked like the devil incarnate under the moon's glow, especially with the ghostly floating of his duster in the breeze.

Stubby said, "Sheeit."

Harley said, "She weren't lyin' 'bout the husband."

Cooper repeated, enunciating each word, "Let her go. Step away. And I might let you live."

Stubby started backing up as Harley slowly removed his hand from Hallie's mouth, released her waist, and lifted his hands in the air.

Cooper motioned with one gun, "Hallie, come over by me."

Hallie jerked away from the wretched man and in the process purposefully jabbed his gut with her elbow. Although he grunted, her angry attempt to inflict pain proved useless on his overweight body.

Rushing to stand behind Cooper, she stared daggers at the men's faces lit by the full moon.

Cooper's calm voice turned menacing. "If I see either one of you even looking sideways at a woman as long as we're on this boat, I'll shoot your hands off, and then I'll gouge your eyes out. Do. I. Make. Myself. Clear?"

His tone sent shivers up Hallie's spine. In the darkness, with moonlight reflecting from the hard planes of his face and his pistols glinting ominously, he could have scared the demons in hell.

Stubby and Harley blubbered simultaneously, evidence of their drunken state seemingly disappeared.

"Y-yes."

"Yes, sir."

Cooper motioned with a jerk of his head. "Get the hell out of my sight."

Neither man waited for a second invitation before stumbling over each other in their haste to retreat.

Much to Hallie's astonishment, Cooper then twirled and holstered his guns like a gunslinger. She had to stop herself from throwing her arms around his neck in grateful abandonment for saving her.

Unable to see his face clearly now because of the angle of his head, she gasped at the anger in his voice when he practically growled, "What the hell are you doing out at this time of night? Especially on this deck."

She opened her mouth to reply, but her explanation got stuck in her throat.

"Well?" he asked impatiently.

"I-I couldn't sleep and wanted to get some fresh air and look at the stars."

Cooper sighed. "Mrs. Wells, if you want me to get you to Oregon intact, you had best listen to my instructions. While we were boarding, I *warned* you about this part of the ship. If I hadn't come along, those men would have done things you don't even want to think about."

Hallie felt the blood drain from her face at the truth in his words and relived the feel of the horrible man's hand groping her. She covered her mouth to keep from vomiting and made a retching sound.

Immediately, Cooper stepped close and pressed a handkerchief into her hand. "Ah, damn. Take some deep breaths. Breathe in...breathe out."

Hallie followed his instructions, mortified that she might throw up in front of him. In all of her life, she had never been manhandled by ruffians or spoken to harshly as Cooper had just done. She was brought up in a loving family and married a dear, sweet-tempered man who never raised his voice. The nausea finally faded.

"Better?" Cooper's voice had softened, but an unreasonable anger crawled into Hallie's heart.

"Yes. I'm ready to return to my cabin," she answered curtly, handing back his handkerchief. She started forward and then turned quickly around. "In the future, Mr. Jerome, I would appreciate it if you wouldn't speak to me as if I were a child. I apologize for my lapse in judgment and I hope that puts an end to this unfortunate conversation."

Turning pridefully she walked toward the stairs.

* * *

Cooper watched Hallie's stiff-backed retreat and almost smiled. So the timid mouse had some spunk. Rather than incense her more—an itch he had to see how far he could push her—he just said, "Yes, ma'am."

Cooper escorted Hallie back to her room and politely tipped his hat when she turned to bid him good night. Still miffed, she asked, "Since that deck houses the card tables and liquor, why were *you* there, Mr. Jerome?"

Her question took him off guard. He knew that if he grinned at her schoolmarm interrogation, he would probably be in the doghouse for days.

"Ah, ma'am, I was just scouting out the lay-of-the-land, so to speak. It's a habit from my military training." His explanation sounded plausible to his own ears, but the look on Hallie's face told him that she knew it was a crock of bull as much as he did. "Night, ma'am. Sorry if I was a little harsh with you." Before she could respond, he hastened away.

Descending to the main deck, Cooper swiped a hand across his nose at the pungent odor of animal excrement and body odor from the mass of emigrants camped there. Making his way to the area set aside for animals, he leaned against the pitiful stall housing Sweet Pea. His horse softly neighed and lifted her head over the siding for her owner to rub. Absentmindedly, Cooper crooned and stroked Sweet Pea's neck while Hallie's question bounced around in his mind. What had he been doing on the hurricane deck? Hell, he'd been wanting a drink and a woman's company, but instead of acting on either desire, he, too, had been stargazing. Chuckling, he dropped to the blanket at his feet, laid his head on his saddle, and pulled the bowl of his hat over his face.

* * *

After spending most of the night unable to sleep, Hallie listened to Timmy's excited chatter the next morning as she dressed. Oh, how she was loathe to face

Cooper. He must think her a total nitwit. What had she been thinking to sneak to the gambling deck by herself? A sudden panic hit her. *What if he decides not to accompany us to Oregon?*

"Ma? Ma…Ma!" Timmy shook her elbow.

"Oh, sorry, honey."

"Whatcha thinkin' 'bout? You been actin' strange since we got up."

"I was just thinking about all the sights we're going to see today," she fibbed.

"I can't wait! Do you 'spose the Hankersons are up yet?"

"I'm sure they are. Let's tidy up and then we'll knock on their door."

"Sure, Ma." Timmy stood on top of her bed so he could reach his own above it and straighten the covers

A sudden burst of love filled Hallie's heart for her precious son and she kissed his cheek. "I love you, Timmy."

Her boy turned and smiled. "I love you, too, Ma. I bet Pa's watchin' us from heaven right now."

Hallie felt the quick stab of tears. "I just bet you're right."

When they exited their stateroom, the Hankersons were already standing on the promenade with Sammy holding his mother's hand while his father locked their door. Sammy saw Timmy and shouted, "Timmy, have you gotten sick from the rocking of the boat? I puked three times last night, but I feel better now."

Timmy made a face. "No. I feel okay. Sure hope I don't puke."

As Hallie greeted her friends, Mr. Hankerson glanced past her. "Hello, Cooper. I hope you slept well."

Mortification flooded Hallie, but she gathered her courage and turned around. Looking rested and having actually shaved his usual growth of dark stubble to reveal an incredibly rugged, but handsome face, Cooper stared at her. It seemed that his blue eyes twinkled and his mouth quirked.

He turned his gaze on Emmett.

"I slept very well, Emmett," and then, with a pointed glance back at Hallie, he finished with, "Fresh air does wonders for a man's sleep."

Hallie's eyes widened. *Is he joking with me? He doesn't seem angry.* Relief tumbled off her shoulders like a flash flood.

Emmet said, "Cooper, we missed you last night, will you join us in the dining room? The food is adequate."

Hallie grinned. "Yes, please join us. It's a lovely day and I forgot to tell you food is included in the ticket price."

"I'd be pleased. As for last night, I got caught up helping families get settled on the main deck and chasing more wayward animals." He chuckled.

Emmett glanced at his wife and Hallie and made a sweeping motion. "Ladies, lead the way."

After a short wait for a table, a waiter led them to a corner with a lovely view. Cooper politely pulled out Hallie's chair and then sat across from her, with Timmy and Sammy on either side of him. Mrs. Hankerson sat next to Hallie with her husband at her other side.

Menus were placed in front of them and Timmy announced, "I'm so hungry my stomach is touching my backbone."

Sammy piped up, "I'm so hungry my belly button is touching my backbone," and everyone laughed. After that, the boys tried to outdo each other in vocal creativity.

They gave their orders to the harried waiter, a young man probably not more than twenty, with slicked back red hair and enough freckles to fill a washtub. He introduced himself as Charlie, confiding that it was his first steamboat job and someday he wanted to captain one.

Over a breakfast of biscuits, sausage gravy, scrambled eggs, cornmeal mush, and strong black coffee, Hallie found herself relaxing and enjoying adult conversation for the first time in a long while. Even when the pastor and church members stopped by to check on her, she hadn't engaged in meaningful conversation. Now, sitting here, she realized how much she missed conversing with Thomas. Being somewhat disabled, he'd read extensively and shared his knowledge with her.

Removing her thoughts from the past, Hallie turned her attention across the table. Cooper lazed back in his chair and looked from Timmy to Sammy. "Did you know that Kit Carson traveled the same trail we're about to embark on? In fact, he was one of the first to map it."

Timmy exclaimed, "Kit Carson! The mountain man all the dime novels are about?"

"The very same."

Sammy asked, "You got any of his stories?"

Cooper chuckled, "Well, now, I just might have one or two in my saddlebag. Would you like to borrow them?" He glanced at Hallie and the Hankersons. "That is, if it's all right."

Hallie smiled. "Perfectly all right."

Emmett said, "I'd love to enjoy them myself. I can read them to the boys."

After that, Timmy and Sammy couldn't stop talking about Kit Carson and his many exploits.

When they rose to leave their table, Hallie reached into her reticule to leave a tip for their young waiter with big dreams. Cooper touched her hand. "No, ma'am. I've got it. You save your money for the journey."

The expression in Cooper's eyes revealed his determination, so she gracefully nodded and followed the others to the promenade. As they stood at the railing watching waves ripple outward from the paddles, Cooper tipped the brim of his hat in a parting gesture. "I'd best check on my horse. I'll see ya'll later." He turned to leave.

Hoping Timmy wouldn't hear while his and Sammy's attention was focused on another steamer farther upriver, Hallie asked softly, "Cooper, may I speak with you privately a moment, please?"

He adjusted his hat and motioned to an empty section of the railing. "Of course, ma'am."

When she was alone with Cooper, Hallie felt suddenly shy. "I-I just want to apologize for my unseemly behavior last night. I should never have left my stateroom. It was foolish and you were right to be angry with—"

Bending at the knees so he was on her level, Cooper interrupted with his gravelly voice; "No, ma'am, I was out of line to speak to you so offensively. I have a quick temper that sometimes gets the better of me. I should be apologizing to you."

Hallie had been avoiding his gaze, but his surprising admission made her glance quickly at him. His face was only inches from hers, and she inhaled sharply, gnawing at her lower lip. Cooper stood straight, again towering over her, and she let her eyes move up his chest to his face. He smiled a lopsided grin. "So, ma'am, let's just put that unpleasant experience behind us."

Numbly, Hallie nodded. Cooper surprised her on every account. Sometimes he seemed as rough as a blasting sand storm and other times, like now, he appeared as gentle as a mare nudging her foal in its first steps. Relief flooded Hallie that he wasn't holding her mistake against her. Glancing at his worn boots, she whispered, "Thank you."

Cooper took a step backward and she looked up to one of his endearing half smiles. Tipping his hat again, he said, "I'll see you later, Hallie," and walked away. He had only taken a couple of steps when he turned back around with a boyish expression. "I was on the deck last night because I was stargazing."

Because he was already walking away again, he didn't see Hallie's smile.

Chapter 8: Westport Bound

The five days it took the *Mirabella* to reach Westport Landing, docking at ports along the way to release and load passengers, cargo, and animals, were days Hallie would later remember with fondness. Little did she realize just how grueling the next five months of her life would become. During the steamboat trip, she met other emigrants bound for her same wagon train under the leadership of Captain Jeremiah J. Jones. Thomas had specifically chosen Captain Jones's train because he was considered one of the finest and most experienced drivers on the trail.

Hallie soon came to realize that the majority of people headed west were families seeking the promise of bountiful lands, beautiful streams teeming with all manner of fish, and better lives for themselves and their children. Of course, scattered amidst the families were businessmen hoping for successful ventures in the new land and prospectors with gold fever.

During her first day on the river, Hallie took inventory of her funds, and although plentiful, her practical nature had her thinking about ways to become even more frugal. While she had often chided Thomas on his tendency to overspend, she would be forever grateful he'd purchased staterooms on the *Mirabella*. He had saved her the harshness of having to sleep on the main deck without benefit of a room or food. The poor women whose husbands were unable to afford first class accommodations, looking haggard and bedraggled, did their best for their families by preparing meals from their own goods and attempting to create privacy by hanging blankets. Hallie felt guilty for having so much when others had so little, and made a mental note to help others as occasions arose.

The closer they came to Westport Landing, the more the banks of the river teemed with emigrants camping alongside it until their wagon trains left. Most trains left by the end of April, weather permitting. The spring grasses were absolutely necessary for the grazing of livestock. Thomas had said that leaving too early was as dangerous as leaving too late and taking the chance of being caught in the winter snows.

Riffling through her trunk, Hallie retrieved a sheet of writing paper, unpacked her ink and quill, and began making lists of the items she would need to purchase. Because prices were higher farther along the trail and the quality less, Cooper said they would purchase everything in Westport.

After a short time, her head started to spin with the immensity of what would be required—flour, cornmeal, rice, sugar, coffee, tea, beans, hardtack, salt pork, tin plates and cups, utensils, blankets, wash tub and scrub board, soap—and those were only a few of the small items. The necessities on her large items and animals list included a sturdy wagon and oxen, milk cow, chickens, tools, and that was just the beginning.

Her head pounding with anxiety, she set her writing aids aside and thought about Thomas's calm demeanor—such a kind man. Tears of loneliness escaped her resolve not to cry and dripped from her chin onto her lists. Sniffling, she did what Thomas always suggested when life became too overwhelming; she closed her eyes, breathed deeply, and envisioned the end from the beginning. She imagined a homey cabin snuggled amidst tall trees and a bubbling creek filling the air with happy, gurgling sounds. She envisioned a bend in the creek and, lifting the skirt of a pretty blue calico dress, skipped around it, laughing…

Hallie's eyes popped wide open. *Hallie, what are you thinking?* She had visualized Cooper fishing with Timmy. When he glanced up and saw her, he handed his pole to Timmy, opened his arms, and waited for her to run into them.

Wiping the vision from her mind, Hallie jumped up, folded her list and stuffed it in her reticule. *Foolish, foolish, woman,* she scolded herself.

Chapter 9: Land Legs

The *Mirabella* docked at Westport Landing in the midst of a downpour. Even so, travelers couldn't wait to depart the ship, especially those who had been making due on the main deck. Standing under the overhang of the promenade, Cooper glanced at Hallie, Timmy, and the Hankersons. "Doesn't look like this weather is going to let up anytime soon, but I'm sure the captain will be shooing us off his ship to prepare for his return trip."

Hallie asked, "Where's Sweet Pea?"

Cooper responded, "I paid one of the older boys of an emigrant family with a passel of kids—ten was my last count—to take him to the closest stable and wait for me."

Hallie frowned. "I'm sure that's an expense you hadn't planned on. I'll reimburse you after we're settled for the day."

Cooper returned Hallie's frown and set his jaw at a now recognizable, stubborn angle. "No, ma'am, I'll not take any money for anything to do with my horse."

"But, Cooper–"

He interrupted; "Ma'am, Sweet Pea is *my* responsibility, and besides, you need everything you've got to outfit yourself for this train."

Sammy glanced back and forth between the two of them. "Aw, do we have to wait for Miz Hallie to buy a dress? We already been standin' here since forever waitin' for the rain to let up."

For a second, the meaning of his words escaped everyone's understanding, but when they realized he had misunderstood Cooper's reference to Hallie "outfitting" herself, the group laughed, easing the tension between them Hallie and Cooper.

While Emmett chuckled and lifted Sammy onto his shoulders, Cooper motioned to two deck hands. "I'll direct these young chaps in delivering your trunks to the dock and will meet ya'll under that blue awning after I hire a buckboard." He pointed across the muddy wharf road to the weathered façade and overhang of a store whose sign, hanging at a precarious tilt, simply said, "Outfitter."

Having decided to continue her financial discussion with Cooper later, Hallie opened her umbrella, acknowledged Cooper with a nod, and grasped Timmy's hand to follow the Hankersons off the ship and across the road.

* * *

Cooper watched Hallie's retreat. The diminutive woman was certainly stubborn. He recognized the set of her shoulders brooked no argument, but hell would freeze over before he'd allow her to shoulder expenses for his horse. His first impression of her as a determined, although easily manipulated woman, had been mightily disproved. From the look in her eyes, he hadn't heard the last about her reimbursing him. He could only imagine her indignation when he refused payment for his services at the end of the journey. When she'd tried to pay him before leaving Jebson, he'd refused her money, pacifying her by saying he wanted to be paid at the end of the trail, after he earned his fee

He chuckled because he knew holy hell was going to break loose at that encounter.

Most people considered him to be as poor as a church mouse, which suited him just fine. In reality, he'd saved over the years and made a few wise investments, but gambling winnings constituted the bulk of his money. And because of the condition of the farm he'd purchased, the money forked out hadn't set him back much at all.

Cooper's amusement faded however when he remembered the reason for his generosity to Hallie. He knew she would want an explanation and he wasn't sure he wanted to admit his failure as a husband and father.

Oh, Jake, I wish I'd been the kind of man your ma could've counted on, even if she couldn't love me. I wish I'd been around to see you grow up."

Regret washed over Cooper more powerfully than the sudden watershed from the dreary clouds. When Marybeth had told him she wanted a divorce, he'd laughed. Divorce simply wasn't done. Once a man was married, he was married for good. He'd changed his mind, however, but it wasn't her tears and pleas that did it; it was walking in on her in bed with the local banker. He'd almost killed the bastard, but Marybeth's shrieks and determination to protect him with her own body made Cooper realize something—she truly loved the gray-haired banker with his handlebar mustache. In fact, the man's own attempt to protect Marybeth at the cost of his own life was another jolt for Cooper—the banker loved Marybeth just as vehemently. After that, there was no way they could stay married. Hell, he hadn't been a good husband or father anyway, what with leaving for long periods to drive herds of longhorns along the Shawnee Trail from Texas to Missouri. Although he always cared for the practical needs of his family, emotionally, he hadn't been there for them.

As for Jake, he loved the boy, but didn't know how to be a father, having been abandoned himself at the age of six by a prostitute mother and raised by an uncle who already had ten kids he liked to beat the daylights out of, with Cooper being his new favorite.

When Cooper turned twenty and met Marybeth, a pretty, black-headed gal with a voluptuous figure, he was smitten by lust…and then love. Her being five years older didn't bother him at all. In fact, it added to her allure. She'd been married in her teens and widowed at the age of twenty-two. To her sadness, she'd had no children with her first husband and desperately wanted them. Cooper was more than happy to oblige, but never having had a father, he soon felt weighted with the responsibility and found himself on the range often. All Marybeth ever wanted was a loving family, and when he thought about it later, he understood her unfaithfulness. The banker was everything Cooper wasn't.

That nasty encounter was the epiphany he needed to give his wife her freedom. Lowering the gun he'd threatened Marybeth and the banker with, he said, "Marybeth, you can have your divorce." After that, he stayed long enough to sign the papers and say goodbye to Jake. Never having spent much time with his father, the three-year-old lifted a chubby hand to wave goodbye and then went back to playing with his wooden horse in the dirt. That was his last memory of his son.

His boy was turning fifteen in a few days and Cooper wasn't the reckless young man he had once been. But it was too late for him and his boy.

Jake was the reason Cooper couldn't accept payment for helping Hallie. In some strange way, helping Hallie and Tim was atonement for the fiasco he had created with Marybeth and Jake. Maybe it didn't make sense, but most of his life hadn't made sense.

Cooper returned his thoughts to the present. *Nope, Hallie, you can fight me tooth and nail, but I won't take a dime of your money.*

Acquiring a buckboard and loading the trunks took quite some time, what with everyone and his brother attempting to do the same thing, but finally, Cooper located the livery, retrieved Sweet Pea and tied her to the back of the buckboard, and then pulled to the front of the Outfitters store where Tim and Emmett leaned against the siding and Lydia and Sammy sat on a bench. He didn't see Hallie.

"Whoa!" he called to the horses, pulling them in front of an adjoining business—a dining room with grimy windows and a lopsided sign tacked near the door that advertised, *Special of the Day—Meatloaf and Tators,* looking like it had been scrawled years earlier. He jumped off the buckboard, looped the reins around the hitching post, and walked toward the store. The Hankersons and Tim met him on the boardwalk.

Tim grinned, the gaping hole of his missing tooth the first thing anyone saw when talking to the boy. "Howdy Mr. Jerome; Ma's in the store checking on supplies."

Cooper almost groaned aloud. He sure hoped the woman wasn't making any purchases. This would be the last place he'd buy necessities—its worn down condition and location making the supplies questionable and the prices exorbitant.

Cooper tipped his hat. "I best check on your ma." He quickly stepped around the boy. Inside the store, he found her engaged in conversation with a greasy geezer who looked to be older than God. He heard her say, "So, Mr. Tucker, you're telling me that you've got the best prices anywhere in the area?"

The old man jawed his tobacco and turned to spit the black stuff in a rusty spittoon. "Yep, little lady, that's what I'm sayin'."

Cooper interrupted. "Er, Hallie, the trunks are loaded and we're ready to leave."

Hallie jumped at his voice and he almost grinned. What was it about him that always startled her?

She acknowledged his presence with, "Thank you, Cooper, I'll be right there." She turned back to the old sidewinder. "I'll keep your words in mind, Mr. Tucker."

Not wanting to lose a sale, the questionable shopkeeper pointedly directed his words at Hallie, not Cooper, "So, what can I do fer ya in the way of supplies?"

Speaking crisply, Hallie responded, "Like I said, sir, I will keep you in mind." She turned, whisked past Cooper, and said under her breath, "Lying old dog."

Cooper coughed, covered his mouth to hide his smile, and followed Hallie out the door.

* * *

After a half hour's wait, the rain let up enough for them to climb onto the buckboard. Shaking water off the tarp covering their trunks and making the best of a wet situation, the Hankersons and Timmy sat in the bed of the wagon. Cooper assisted Hallie to the front of the buckboard and easily spanned her waist with his large hands. Hallie sucked a breath when his touch seemed to linger a might longer than necessary, but then she decided she was just imagining it. In her mind, Cooper was the kind of man who went for tall, buxom women, probably saloon gals, not timid, plain, skinny, country women. Again, she chastised herself for letting her mind wander. Why her thoughts kept drifting into the forbidden zone, she had no idea. She turned her attention to what Cooper was saying.

"I asked around and found out there's a decent hotel in the heart of town. Also, we'll probably want to shop prices on supplies. After I get you and Tim settled in the hotel, I'll start making inquiries about oxen and a wagon." He lowered his voice. "Um, excuse me if I'm being indiscreet, but are we still working with the same availability of funds you divulged to me in Jebson, ma'am?"

Hallie lowered her own voice. "Oh, yes, of course. I have four thousand dollars from the sale of my farm and another thousand remaining in savings after Thomas purchased our land in Oregon."

Cooper nodded. "That relieves my mind. I think I'll be able to outfit you very well and get your cabin built in Oregon."

Hallie leaned closer and said softly, "Please don't forget your wages, sir. Whatever you would have profited on the sale of your crops…and a little more, should be fair."

Hallie got the feeling Cooper was amused when he responded, "Yes, ma'am." But he sounded serious when he continued, "You know, a woman running a farm alone is risky business."

Hallie sighed. "Yes, I realize that, but as I explained during our initial meetings, because of his disability, my husband was unable to do the manual labor associated with planting and harvesting, so we hired hands specifically for those tasks. Because we paid them well, they did an excellent job. And except for one year with inclement weather, we always made a tidy profit come harvest time. My husband was a very astute planner and I was prudent with our funds. And if there's one thing I know how to do, it's farm. So, having said all that, I have no doubt I can continue that same practice. I have enough funds to keep me going until the first harvest and possibly beyond. Of course, I realize there are always unknowns in any equation, but I must fortify my courage and continue on. Farming is what I know and what I love. So please, Mr. Jerome, do not trouble yourself on my account."

She heard Cooper puff a breath and decided to change the subject. Turning to look at his profile, she asked a question that had been on her mind for some time. "Cooper, I'd like to ask you something."

He faced her. "Shoot."

His response made her smile. "You always call my son Tim, never Timmy, like everyone else. I was just wondering why."

Cooper studied her eyes for a second and then returned his gaze to the road. Maneuvering the reins, he guided the horses around a bend before responding. When he did, his answer surprised her.

"Well, Hallie, I'll tell you why, but you may not like what I have to say."

Hallie furrowed her forehead, then said hesitantly, "Please continue."

Cooper readjusted his hat, which sent splashes of water onto the floorboard and sprinkles across Hallie's skirt. Finally, he spoke. "Your boy may be young, Hallie, but he's havin' to grow up fast. Calling him Timmy is like…well…not lettin' him grow up…like keepin' him a toddler. Now the name Tim, it's a man's name, something your boy is going to become faster because of losin' his pa." Cooper paused, and Hallie saw him glance at her profile and then back at the road. "I hope you understand what I'm trying to say. I don't mean any offense."

Hallie fingered a tear, turning so that Cooper could only see the back of her head. When she felt like her voice wouldn't tremble, she looked straight ahead again and replied, "I do understand. Thank you for telling me. I'm going to ponder your words and talk to Timmy…" she smiled slightly, "…Tim …about what you've said."

Unexpectedly, Cooper reached and covered her hands folded tightly in her lap with one of his big ones. The contact only lasted a second, but it comforted Hallie.

Chapter 10: Gee Haw

Over the next few days, Hallie's mind swam with all the information she'd gleaned from Cooper, Emmett, and other emigrants flooding Westport. The town was a beehive of activity from sunrise until well after sundown. The list of supplies she began on the *Mirabella* was revised and added to daily. She now had quantities to add to some entries. Early one morning, while Tim still slept, she took advantage of first light and sat beside the window reviewing her list.

Glancing at her son, she smiled when she thought about how well he'd taken to being called Tim. As gently as she could, she tried to explain what Cooper had said, but Timmy interrupted, "Ma, I been wantin' to be called Tim since Mr. Jerome started callin' me that. Timmy is a baby's name, but I was afraid I'd hurt your feelings if I told you not to call me that anymore."

After their conversation, he informed Sammy that he wanted to be called Tim, and Sammy responded with, "Then I want to be called Sam."

Hallie was fearful that Emmett and Lydia would become offended, but when she explained, they agreed wholeheartedly. Emmett declared, "Sammy, you are now officially Sam because this journey is going to grow you up, too."

Hallie returned her thoughts to her rewritten list.

500 pounds flour
400 pounds smoked bacon

150 pounds lard
120 pounds hardtack
75 pounds sugar
50 pounds coffee
50 pounds rice
50 pounds beans
10 pounds salt
2 pounds tea
5 gallons whiskey
vinegar
dried fruit
dried vegetables
saleratus
parched corn
corn meal (also for packing eggs)

Hallie sighed. This was just the food. Turning to the next list, she read:

Washtub
Washboard
Flatiron and starch
Soap
Coffee grinder
Coffee pot
Utensils
Skillet
Pots and pans
Dutch oven
Reflector oven
Lanterns
Candles

Tripod

Buckets

Canteens

Water barrels

Sewing supplies

Shovel, pick axe, hammer, hatchet, saw, other tools

Hallie paused to gaze out the window. The tedious task of reviewing her lists was forgotten in the beauty of daybreak. Pink suffused the eastern sky with golden streaks fanning outward like loving fingers attempting to touch the soil. Imagining the moment she would step onto her land brought a smile and quiet laughter, and she whispered, "Five more days and we leave for Oregon."

She lifted her eyes to the pink heavens. "Tom, I just want you to know Cooper is taking good care of us. He's been haggling with the merchants and getting the best prices for the best goods. He doesn't settle for seconds. Sometimes I argue with him over wanting to load the wagon with more supplies, but he swears overloading is the worst thing we could do." She paused, glanced at Tim, still snoring, and then back at the painted sky. "I trust him, Tom."

* * *

Cooper examined the seven oxen. They looked to be sturdy, well fed, and dependable. He wanted this team but the price being asked was still too high. Pursing his lips, he eyeballed the stable owner with a direct stare and the man's return gaze didn't waver. Cooper decided he was an honest man. "Two hundred and forty-five dollars is still too high. I'll give you two hundred."

The leather-faced old merchant pulled on a strand of his gray beard that fanned out over his chest. "Nope. You're too low. These are some of the finest oxen in Westport. Hell, make that Independence *and* Westport." He cocked his head at an angle and pulled on his beard again. "Two hundred and twenty-five dollars. That's with a price break on the extra ox."

Cooper glanced back at the oxen, walked around them, felt them again, and grinned when his back was to the old fart. Wiping the grin off his face, he turned back around and stuck out his hand. "You strike a mean bargain, Mr. Piper, but I'll pay your price."

After paying half the amount as earnest money, Cooper made arrangements to pick the oxen up the day they left. He grinned at his good fortune. So far, the day had yielded oxen and a wagon. The prairie schooner he'd purchased for one hundred dollars was premium quality and the seller had thrown in a bucket of grease and spare parts, including spokes and an axle. The canvas had been well oiled with linseed to make it waterproof and the wheels were wide, making for easier travel in sandy soils.

Yep, Cooper was happy with his purchases and looked forward to the smile that would light Hallie's face when he told her.

Four days before departure, Hallie sat beside Cooper on their rented buckboard while the Hankersons and Tim rode in the back. Postings on the community wall and in the local newspaper had informed anyone bound for the trail with Wagon Train Master Captain

Jeremiah J. Jones to meet in front of City Hall for the purpose of discussing "Important Particulars," and also to take a headcount.

Hallie's heart raced; soon she would be traveling to a new state, a new home, and new beginnings. Excitement and fear of the unknown vied for preeminence of her emotions. Calming herself with slow breaths, she glanced sideways at Cooper. His expertise in negotiating the best deals on the best supplies made her forever grateful to him. Since the night on the boat when he'd spoken harshly to her, he hadn't brought up the incident again, and his manner was always patient and gentlemanly, quite in contrast to his rough appearance. Remembering his treatment of the two cowpokes who had accosted her and his wielding of not one, but two pistols, as if such behavior were an often occurrence, she tried to reconcile that man with the one beside her—a man who was kind to animals and respectful of women.

The braking of the buckboard brought Hallie back to the present and she glanced across the street at the gathering crowd, excitement overcoming her fear. She couldn't wait for a glimpse of Captain Jones. Cooper lead her across the street holding her elbow while she held Tim's, who after their conversation about his name, informed her that only babies held their mother's hand.

A platform, no doubt for politicians and city leaders to address the public, had been built in front of the steps to City Hall and Cooper directed them to an open space on one side of it.

While they waited for Captain Jones, Hallie glanced at the emigrants filling the square. Such an assortment of people she had never seen altogether in one place. Most of the pioneers were families with children of every age—babies to adults. She was surprised by the number of older husbands and wives and it made her smile. *Just goes to show you're never too old to seek adventure and new beginnings.*

Among the crowd, she noted a gathering of "fancy women," their colorful satin bodices revealing generous cleavages and their decorative hats with feathers showcasing upswept hairstyles in startling contrast to the plain bonnets and buns of the country women, herself included. Moving her gaze past them, she stiffened when she recognized the slimy cowboys who had accosted her—Stubby and his cohort, Harley.

Glancing at Cooper, she saw that he, too, had spotted them. His eyes, as hard and cold as lead shot on a frosty morning, sent chills up her spine. When she returned her gaze to Stubby and Harley, she saw Harley elbowing his friend and pointing in her direction. Stubby turned and his eyes widened, forcing his forehead into grimy creases. Hallie was close enough to read Stubby's lips as he mouthed, "Sheeit!" Saying something to Harley, he made a flapping motion with one hand and the two of them edged to the outermost grouping of people.

Cooper bent down to her. "Rest assured, Hallie, they won't even glance in your direction after I have another talk with them."

Hallie couldn't help but laugh. "I think you've already put the fear of God in them just with your expression. Thank you."

Cooper laughed also. "I've never been thanked for my ugly mug, but I'll make sure to keep it pointed in their direction throughout the journey."

Ugly mug? Hallie nearly objected—vehemently, but then realized how improper it would be to tell him how handsome she thought him to be.

A wave of excitement rolled through the crowd, bringing Hallie's attention to the platform when a man, probably in his fifties and dressed in military attire, jumped up on the wooden dais. He looked to be as tall and muscular as the storybook character, Paul Bunyan. His booming voice reminded her of cracking thunder when he shouted, "Listen up, pioneers! I'm Captain Jeremiah J. Jones and I proudly served in the Union army. Now that the war is over, I still serve my country as a civilian consultant, but I'm back to doin' what I do best—makin' sure ya'll reach your destinations in one piece. So, that bein' said, I've got instructions that need to be followed exactly as I give 'em. Anyone wantin' to rebel might as well find another train to hitch up with. I'm a mean wagon master when it comes to givin' orders and I don't take no sass!" He paused for effect and then bellowed, "Is that understood?" When the intimidated crowd didn't answer, the captain yelled, "Is that understood?"

Cooper was the first to call out, "Yes, sir. Your leadership is legendary. I, for one, understand."

After that, men, women, and children nodded and affirmed—almost of one accord— "Yes, sir."

The captain continued, "Good. I always like gettin' that out of the way first. Now about those 'Important Particulars.' In a minute I'm going to tell you where to relocate your wagons after they're loaded, what to pack, and acceptable behavior on the trail. But before I do, I want to reinforce the fact that your life and the lives of your fellow travelers depend on you followin' instructions. And here's one more admonishment, "DO NOT OVERPACK OR YOU WILL END UP DUMPIN' YOUR GOODS ALONGSIDE THE TRAIL!"

Pointedly, Captain Jones glared from person to person. He asked loudly, "Is that understood?"

In concert, the pioneers quickly affirmed, "Yes, sir!"

Hallie held her hand to her heart. The wagon master was the most fearsome man she had ever encountered. She glanced from beneath her lashes to see Cooper's reaction. Whereas Captain Jones scared the daylights out of her, an amused smile played across Cooper's lips. *Does nothing and no one scare him?*

* * *

For the next two days, Cooper, with Hallie and Tim accompanying him, drove their buckboard to different merchants to pay for food staples, tools, and a passel of other supplies. Cooper estimated their load would be around nineteen hundred pounds, well within the higher limit of twenty-five hundred pounds, tops, instructed by Captain Jones.

On the third day he returned to the businesses to load their prairie schooner with their purchases, and, feeling satisfied with their cargo, met Hallie and Tim in front of their hotel. The final item to be loaded was Hallie's trunk. Tossing a coin to a strong looking boy for assistance, the two of them loaded it, and after a final inspection of the wagon and oxen, milk cow and his own horse, Cooper turned to Tim. "Are you ready?"

"Oh, yes, sir!"

He glanced at Hallie. "What about you?"

"You know I am." A sudden softness overcame her features. "I can't thank you enough. Without you, we wouldn't have accomplished this."

Cooper glanced away from the admiration in her eyes. Whether she knew it or not, right now her feelings were easy to discern, and she was having feelings for him. Hell, the last thing he needed was a complication in his life. He had to stay focused on his mission— deliver Hallie and Tim to Oregon, get them settled, and then return post haste to Missouri. Entanglements with a woman and her kid were not options and the feelings he was having for her scared the bejesus out of him. After the fiasco of his marriage, he was a loner and intended to stay that way.

Turning back to face her, he recognized her hurt expression by him not acknowledging her heartfelt thank you. He smiled slightly. "You're very welcome, Mrs. Wells, but thank-yous are not necessary." *There, calling her Mrs. Wells should get my point across.*

Raising his whip, he slapped it in the air and called, "Giddup." Glancing back around at Hallie and Tim, he nodded, and they began the first mile on foot of their over two thousand mile journey.

* * *

Following a well-worn road behind other prairie schooners traveling to the Cave Spring campsite Captain Jones had designated, Hallie marveled at the numbers headed west though Cooper said the numbers had significantly dwindled from its heyday in the 1840s and 50s. Alongside the road emigrants set up camp in every imaginable apparatus. Some slept in the open, some in tents, some in magnificent schooners like her own, some in rehabilitated farm wagons. And everywhere there were animals: oxen, cows, mules, horses, chickens, dogs, and an occasional cat.

But, oh, the smells: soggy earth from a recent rain, animal dung, flowering trees, spring grasses, even the odor of pioneers needing a bath. When a cool morning breeze lifted the odors, mingled them, and pushed them across the road, Hallie pressed her handkerchief to her nose just as Cooper turned around. He laughed at her squeamishness, cracked his whip, and yelled, "Haw," to correct the animals to the left. Then he called "Gee" because he'd overcorrected them. Finally he got them moving straight ahead.

Hallie wished she hadn't shown her distaste for the blended fragrance, for surely it was to become part and parcel of their journey. Removing her handkerchief, she hoped to redeem herself by appearing indifferent.

Cave Spring was located two miles outside of Westport and many of the pioneers, including the Hankersons, had already arrived. Cooper followed the hand signals of one of their fellow travelers and pulled their schooner to the backside of the one ahead of it forming the wagons into a circle.

Tim asked, "Why are we making a circle? Why can't we just camp where we want?"

Hallie listened to Cooper's reply. "Because forming a circle encloses the animals when necessary and keeps them from escaping. Also, it's protection from wild animals. It's also great for gatherings and holding meetings, which I suspect Captain Jones will do after everyone's arrived."

It was late afternoon before the last wagon completed the campsite, making a total of fifteen in an inner circle and twenty-seven in an outer one, with somewhere around two hundred and fifty people. Just as Cooper had predicted, Captain Jones, looking as fearsome as ever, walked around the wagons and boomed, "Listen up, pioneers! Finish whatever you're doing and meet me in the center of the circle in one hour!"

Hallie and Lydia, who had fried bacon and warmed beans in a pot hung on a tripod over the fire at Hallie's wagon, hastened to pack a loaf of bread away and clean dishes while the men continued readying for the following morning's departure.

In exactly one hour, all the pioneers gathered to hear what Captain Jones had to say. Hallie noticed that Stubby and Harley's dismal looking wagon and pathetic animals were almost directly across from where she was standing, and when she glanced at Stubby, he quickly averted his gaze. Unexpected rage suffused her heart and she wanted to stomp over and slap him. How dare he treat a woman the way he had treated her!

"Listen up, pioneers!" the captain called.

Muffled sounds of talk and laughter suddenly ceased and everyone directed their attention toward Captain Jones. So intimidating was his presence that even children halted their antics and quieted.

"I've called ya'll together to appoint some leaders. I've been checkin' ya'll out, talkin' amongst ya, and here are my decisions." He lifted a paper and began calling off names. "Theodore Tackman, Frank Jensen, Hardy MacIntosh, and Cooper Jerome, please step to the center."

The men stepped forward and Hallie smiled inwardly. She just *knew* Cooper would be one of the men chosen.

Captain Jones pointedly scanned the crowd, causing some folks to shrink backward when he stared directly at them. Loudly, he announced, "These men are my right-handers and I'll be choosing several more in the next few days. When I give my leaders instructions to give to you," he paused for effect, "you *will* obey. Have I made myself clear?"

As they had become accustomed to doing, the crowd responded collectively, "Yes, sir."

Captain Jones smiled, but it did little to soften his stern countenance. "Good." He repeated, "good." After that, he instructed everyone to be ready to leave one hour after daylight on the following day. Then he gave specific instructions regarding safety precautions. He finished by saying, "We'll travel as far as the Shawnee Mission and then camp for the night. Now, except for the men whose names I called earlier, ya'll can return to your wagons and continue your preparations."

Tim tugged on her skirt. "Ma, can I go with Sam so we can look at the pictures in the book again?"

Standing beside Hallie, Lydia said, "I don't mind. In fact, I'd welcome his company to keep Sam distracted."

Hallie gave her permission and watched the Hankersons and her son walk in the direction of their schooner. Cooper was speaking with the captain. Mentally ticking off tasks she still wanted to accomplish before sunset, she started toward her own campsite. She had to pass several women and paused when one of them introduced herself. "Hello, my name is Sarah Jackson and I couldn't help but notice that your husband was chosen by the captain to be a leader. I'm pleased to meet you. Let me introduce you to the rest of these ladies."

Hallie smiled in return, happy to meet other women who would become her traveling companions for over two thousand miles. She stuck out her hand. "I'm pleased to meet you, Sarah Jackson. My name is Hallie Wells, but you must call me Hallie, and Mr. Jerome isn't my husband."

A confused expression passed across Sarah's face. "I'm sorry. I just assumed you two were married."

Uh oh. Hallie hadn't considered the effect her introduction would have on the ladies. "Uh, Mr. Jerome is driving my wagon to Oregon because of the recent passing of my husband."

Relief washed over Sarah's face and Hallie thought, *That was simple enough.*

Unexpectedly, another woman in the group stepped forward, her face seemingly frozen in a sneer. "So, you're traveling with a man who isn't your husband?"

Hallie blinked, surprised at her hateful tone. "Yes, ma'am. But as I just explained, my husband recently passed and…"

Ignoring Hallie's explanation, the woman snorted, *"Proper women* do not travel with men they are not married to, no matter the explanation. My name is

Prudence Pittance and I am the wife of Pastor Pittance. These ladies are part of our congregation and until you are properly escorted, we will *not* associate with you. Come, ladies."

Hallie watched the women's expressions, so welcoming at first, transform into pity on some and hostility on others. Mrs. Pittance lifted her black skirt and, with exaggerated movement, turned her back on Hallie and stomped away. The other women followed her example. Sarah was the last to leave, giving Hallie a tiny, apologetic smile.

So shocked was Hallie by the event that she remained motionless, attempting to process what had just transpired. Her first reaction was a desire to cry because she had never been treated thus in her life. In another instant, anger welled up in her heart. *How dare she judge me!*

Lifting her skirts in indignation, Hallie turned toward her wagon and saw Cooper watching her from the center of the circle. Had he witnessed that horrible confrontation?

Chapter 11: "Westward Ho!"

Cooper walked to Hallie's wagon and turned his attention to checking the wheel spokes. Unfortunately, he had heard prune-faced Mrs. Pittance chastising her. *Damn, I knew this was going to happen.*

Not wanting to embarrass Hallie further, he pretended ignorance of their encounter. In just a short time around Hallie, he'd come to realize that for all her bravado, she was a sheltered woman, not familiar with the unkindness of people—well, at least until now. Cooper, however, had learned to shrug off the bitterness that clung to holier-than-thou contentious people like a creeping vine, having been raised around them.

He felt a protective streak wanting to sprout and tried to kill it. Safeguarding Hallie physically was one thing; shielding her emotionally was out of the question. Helping her because of Tim he could handle. Allowing her to get under his skin was absolutely unacceptable.

Walking away from the wagon, he resolved to remain detached and decided to check on Sweet Pea.

* * *

Hallie woke long before dawn and waited to hear the first stirrings of pioneers before rising. Dressing quickly and slipping from her wagon, she was grateful she had harkened to Cooper's wisdom and not overloaded it, leaving plenty of room for herself and Tim. Unless absolutely necessary, she had no intention of sleeping on the ground. Besides, she didn't want to give the gossip mongers more to wag their tongues about.

Turning her gaze away from Prudence Pittance's wagon, she prayed quietly, "Lord, give me patience. Keep my tongue from speaking evil and my heart from being bitter against that woman." But even as she prayed, Hallie knew she was fighting a losing battle. She already harbored bad feelings. Forcing her thoughts to more important matters, she stoked the fire Cooper had already started.

The sun crested on a beautiful, chilly morning. With campfires sprouting around the circle, the camp began to hum with excitement as women prepared breakfast, men prepared their modes of transportation, small children played, older children cared for their family's animals, and Captain Jones circled inside and outside the camp on his gelding, his sharp eyes on constant alert and his tongue calling out orders.

A frisson of excitement skated up Hallie's spine. Like herself, this was the day many of the pioneers had been anticipating for months, possibly years.

Pulling the reflector oven, cast iron skillet, and necessary utensils from their crate, she instructed Tim to unpack a pound of salted bacon from its storage in the wheat barrel. Cooper said he'd learned on cattle drives that bacon preserved longer and less fat melted on hot days if stored in that manner. Again, Hallie felt thankful for his presence and wondered about his life before joining the military.

Before long, she had biscuits baking, bacon sizzling, and, after it turned crispy, eggs frying in bacon grease. Pleased with her efforts, she asked Tim to find Cooper and let him know breakfast was ready.

From sunup until departure, the time taken was about an hour and a half, and when Captain Jones made his final check, he called, "We're half an hour behind schedule. Look lively, people!" Trotting his horse to the lead wagon handled by Hardy MacIntosh, one of his chosen leaders, he boomed in a voice as loud as a foghorn, "Westward Ho!"

Standing behind Cooper, Hallie laughed and turned to Tim beside her. With tears of joy, mingled with tears of sadness that Thomas hadn't lived to experience his dream, she whispered, "Tim, we're on our way."

Her son's eyes clouded with his own tears. "Pa would be right proud, Ma."

Hallie allowed herself one last sniffle, smiled at Tim, and asked, "Son, can we hold hands just this once as we begin our journey?"

Without hesitation, Tim grabbed his mother's hand. "I'd like that, Ma."

Cooper turned around and winked. "Here we go." Lifting his whip, he cracked it in the air above the oxen and shouted "Giddup!" Hallie squeezed Tim's hand and they both laughed as the train started forward.

For the next three hours Tim and Hallie speculated about their land in Oregon, played word games, and teased each other. Then unexpectedly, the wagons in front of them came to a halt. Captain Jones rode the length of the train informing everyone that a mule had thrown a shoe. During the interim to re-shoe the animal, husbands assisted family members from their schooners, though most of the pioneers had walked alongside their wagons so as to not overtax their animals. After a half hour's stopover, the train resumed its plodding progress.

At the noon hour, Captain Jones halted the wagons again, but did not motion them into a circle. He simply rode the length calling out a two-hour break for lunch.

Cooper glanced at Hallie. "When we leave, I think you should ride in the wagon and save your feet. It's best to begin slow."

Hallie paused in slicing bread, attempting to keep her weight off her foot that now had blisters. "If you think so, okay."

Cooper stared pointedly at her feet. "I think so."

After warming beans over the fire that Cooper had started, she handed him a plate of food, but he said, "Feed Tim first." Hallie called to Tim visiting the boys in the wagon ahead of theirs and then dished Cooper's plate. While she scooped beans for herself, several ladies led by Prudence Pittance stomped to her wagon. Hallie recognized two of the women from the day before, but three more were new to her.

Cooper had stepped to the back of the wagon and now rested his hip on the tailgate. Mrs. Pittance glanced toward him and her lip curled into a snarl, but she said nothing, choosing to turn her gaze on Hallie. With a sniff that stuck her nose in the air, she announced, "Mrs. Wells, my ladies and I have a request to make of you."

Her words surprised Hallie. What could they want from her? Keeping her dislike for the woman out of her voice, she responded, "What is that, Mrs. Pittance?"

The distasteful woman lifted a haughty eyebrow, glanced at the women surrounding her wearing the same haughty expressions, and said, "We would like your wagon to travel at the rear of the train, as well as the wagon with the strumpets. Since you are currently in sixth position, your wicked ways are visible for all to see. If you traveled at the rear, the God-fearing folk on this journey would be spared from watching your sinful living with this man."

Hallie's mouth gaped and her eyes widened. From the corner of her eye she saw Cooper push off the wagon and step forward.

The voice of Captain Jones startled everyone. "Well, now, Miz Pittance, when did you become the leader of my train?"

Prudence turned her hateful gaze from Hallie to the captain, seemingly invincible. She sneered, "I was going to speak with you privately, Captain Jones, but since you are here, I will take you to task now." She paused for effect and pushed her tall, stiff frame into even more ramrod straightness before continuing. "I find it appalling, sir, that you have allowed such audacious behavior to run rampant on this train of families traveling west to continue their God-fearing, decent lives, and promote the Good Word." Her voice rose in volume. "Not only have you allowed this man and woman to travel together unmarried, without a chaperone, you have…" she paused again with a face so red and contorted it was frightful, "…you have allowed strumpets and forty-niners to mingle among the good folk. I simply cannot…"

Hallie saw Cooper return to lazing against the wagon. She blinked. He was almost smiling as he glanced back and forth between Mrs. Pittance and Captain Jones.

The sudden boom of the captain's voice sounded like a clap of thunder. "WOMAN! I'VE HEARD ENOUGH!"

Hallie gasped; even Mrs. Pittance's austere expression wavered for a second. She opened her mouth, most likely to lambast Captain Jones again, but he said, "I am the leader of this train! In fact..." he craned his neck toward her, "you can call me God as far as that leadership is concerned!"

Mrs. Pittance and her group of ladies gasped and placed their hands over their hearts. Two of the women appeared about to swoon and were steadied by the others. For once, Mrs. Pittance looked dumbstruck.

Staring first at Mrs. Pittance and then at each woman in turn, Captain Jones said in a softer voice that in some ways was more frightful than his booming one, "If you accost Mrs. Wells again, or *anyone* traveling on *my* train, *you* and your group will be the ones bringing up the rear." Shocked silence hovered like fog, and then the captain shouted, "DO I MAKE MYSELF CLEAR?"

Hallie's own hand covered her breast, not only because of his words, but because of his commanding personage. Sliding her gaze to Cooper, she saw an out-and-out grin plastered across his face.

The captain pointed to the two women unsteady on their feet. "Cooper, help these ladies back to their wagons."

Cooper's smile vanished, but he did not argue. Mrs. Pittance, with eyes as round as saucers, opened her mouth to speak, but Captain Jones raised his hand to stop her. "The rear of the train eats the most dust." He then turned his horse and galloped away.

Mrs. Pittance sputtered and when Cooper stepped forward to assist her ladies, she said, "Don't touch them! We take care of our own!"

Cooper raised his hands in mock surrender and backed away.

Dumbfounded by the events of the past five minutes, Hallie stood rooted to the spot. Then she thought about Tim and scanned the area. He stood off to the side, his eyes as wide as hers.

* * *

In Cooper's estimation, nothing could top the showdown he'd witnessed that day. He'd been so angry at the preacher woman that he'd intended to give her an earful. However, when the captain stepped in, he knew the fiery Mrs. Pittance was about to get burned.

Neither Hallie nor the other pioneers knew that Cooper had served under Captain Jones's military command for a short time. Cooper didn't see any reason to advertise his previous acquaintance with the captain, and obviously Captain Jones felt the same way. After the captain had selected him as one of his leaders they'd met later at the saloon in Westport and reminisced old times. Captain Jones had noticed Cooper drinking sarsaparilla and commented, "I'm glad to see you quit drinkin' that rot gut."

Cooper took a draw on his drink and replied, "If I hadn't, I'd be six feet under right now."

"Ain't that the truth. I gave it up years ago, meself." The captain laughed. "Shall I order us another round of sissy drinks?"

It was late afternoon when they reached the Shawnee Mission and camped south of several buildings built by Methodist missionaries. While Cooper cared for the animals, Tim pulled pots and pans from their crate at his mother's direction. As she was laying firewood, Cooper watched her movements to see how she was faring after the afternoon's confrontation. Her countenance seemed none the worse for Mrs. Pittance's words and he breathed a sigh of relief when she laughed at something Tim said.

Leaving the care of the animals, he joined Hallie and Tim and teased, "You two are having quite a laugh. Is it anything I can be privy to?"

Hallie placed a hand over her mouth, covering her giggle, and pointed to the milk canister hanging on the side of the wagon. "We've got butter churned into a ball in the center of the can from all the jostling of the wagon."

Tim pointed toward the chickens in their cage. "And I said I sure hope we don't have loco chickens after all that jostling." He moved his finger in a circular motion beside his head for emphasis.

Cooper laughed loudly and slapped his leg. He added to the fun, "Loco fried chicken and biscuits dripping with wagon churned butter."

The three of them laughed so loudly that families in the wagons closest to them looked in their direction.

Cooper reached in his pocket for his match tin, got the fire started, and then went back to tending the animals and brushing his horse. While he was checking Sweet Pea's shoes, he heard a woman's concerned cry from across the circle. "Oh, my! There's Injuns!"

Cooper glanced up to see Captain Jones escorting four middle-aged Shawnees to the center of camp: two women and two men. The captain called out, "Listen up, folks. This here is Big Bear and his wife Falling Star, and Red Wolf and his wife Little Elk Sees." He pointed to each person as he named them. "Now, I been friends with them for years. The women make jewelry to sell to pioneers passing this way and their prices are reasonable, so if you've a mind to buy somethin', now's a good time. Charges for everything gets higher the farther west we travel." He turned a meaningful stare toward the Pittance group. "I expect my *friends* to be treated with the utmost respect. Does everyone understand?"

The pioneers nodded and answered, "Yes, sir."

Even at a distance, Cooper could see the scowl that darkened Mrs. Pittance's expression. He shook his head, wondering how someone could turn so hateful. Returning his gaze to the Indians—dressed for effect, a good marketing strategy—he admired their colorfully beaded buffalo skin clothing, feather dressed hair, and ornate necklaces. Some of the pioneers who were already used to trading with Indians hastened to greet them and haggle prices. Cooper watched Hallie biting her bottom lip, alerting him that she was nervous, and wondered what she was thinking. As he watched, she said something to Tim, motioned for him to wait for her, and then joined the group bargaining with the Indians. Cooper smiled as he saw her speak warmly to the women while the men, Indians and whites, stepped to the side to discuss other matters. Within minutes, she was exclaiming over the necklaces, and after several more minutes, she reached into her pocket and slipped out a coin to trade for the treasure she had found. Smiling happily, she thanked the women and returned to camp.

Cooper pushed away from the wagon and said, "It must be pretty, 'cause it's sure got you smiling."

"It's absolutely beautiful. Such talent these women possess to create these intricate designs." She lifted the necklace and drew it over the top of her bonnet to settle against her heart. "I love it because it will always remind me of my journey west."

The smile on her face made Cooper want to buy a cargo load of the necklaces for her, but realizing the inappropriateness of his thoughts, he said, "Looks nice," and quickly turned to find another chore to occupy his time.

When supper was ready, Hallie called to Cooper and handed him a plate heaping with boiled potatoes smothered in the butter they'd laughed about earlier. She also generously loaded his plate with flatbread, salt pork, and pickled green beans.

After supper, Hallie and Tim seemed to melt before Cooper's eyes. Although they had ridden in the wagon for a goodly portion of the day's walk, they weren't used to such activity and Cooper knew it would take a few days for them to get into the swing of things. Hell, *he* wasn't used to all that walking. Wisely, Captain Jones wasn't pushing the emigrants, knowing they needed to build their stamina for the coming months. Before bedding down beside the wagon, Cooper checked their rig and animals one more time.

Shortly before sunrise, he stretched and listened to the animals and pioneers waking to a new day. His back protested when he lifted himself off the hard ground and he chastised himself for getting soft. Quickly rolling his bedding and tying it to the side of the wagon, he got the fire started and the coffee going.

By the time Hallie and Tim exited the wagon he was squatting beside the fire and pouring his first cup. "Good mornin' ma'am; Tim." He raised his cup in their direction. "Coffee's hot, strong, and delicious. Can I pour you some?"

Hallie responded, "Oh, yes, please!"

Tim gave his mother a hopeful look and she said, "You can have half a cup, son."

"Thanks, Ma. Do you want me to pull the skillet out for breakfast?"

"I do. And then gather six eggs out of their cornmeal packing." She ruffled his hair. "And do be gentle so they don't break."

Cooper handed Hallie her coffee and set Tim's on a nearby rock until he returned from his errands.

Hallie sat on the chair Cooper had made sure to include with their supplies and sipped her coffee. Early light suffused the campground and she asked, "Did you sleep well?"

"Yes, ma'am. Yourself?"

"I fear I was so tired not even a stampede would have awakened me."

Cooper laughed at her confession. "Your body will adjust and become stronger in a few days."

She kicked a stone at her feet and said hesitantly, "About what happened yesterday with the preacher lady…"

When she paused, Cooper interjected, "Some unfortunate people have yet to learn respect or human kindness—even if they profess to be God-fearing folk. For myself, I don't pay them no nevermind. But for a fine lady like yourself to be subjected to that…it makes me mad. Captain Jones answered that woman better than anyone could have."

Hallie nodded and they sat silent for a few minutes.

Cooper spoke again as if there had been no pause. "But that woman, dead set as she is in her determination, will more'n likely keep nitpicking and gossiping."

Hallie sighed. "I know. I just hate for Tim to be subjected to such rubbish."

"I wouldn't worry too much about him. He's a strong boy, seeins' as how he's adjusting to losing his pa. He'll be okay."

Cooper's heart constricted when Hallie glanced up, her eyes bright with unshed tears. Wanting to change the subject, he said, "The next notable stop is the Wakarusa River."

Hallie's face lit with interest. "How far are we from there?"

"Two or three days."

Tim, who had just joined them, handed his mother a tin bowl with eggs cushioned by a towel, and asked excitedly, "Are we gonna ride the wagons across the river?"

Cooper laughed. "No. There's a ferry for crossing over. In the early days of the trail, however, the pioneers did a lot of river crossings without the aid of ferries or bridges, son." He immediately realized his slip-of-the-tongue in calling Tim "son," and quickly turned from Hallie's gaze. "Guess I best start getting ready for the day." He hastened to yoke the oxen.

* * *

As the wagons began pulling away from the grassy flatland, the Indian women, along with several children and younger women, watched their departure from the side of the road, smiling and waving. Hallie felt ashamed of her previous wariness of these kind people and waved farewell in return. Touching the lovely necklace lying against her breast, she whispered to her dead husband, "Tom, I've just had a grand experience."

Although Hallie now had blisters on both feet, the ointment she had applied the night before helped and she felt stronger today. The blue sky, puffy clouds, gentle breeze, and Cooper walking ahead of her, cracking the whip above the animals and calling "Gee," or "Haw," depending on the direction he wanted them to go, lifted her spirit into the heavens.

Tim must have felt the same because he loped beside her, kicking stones and bending over to pick up interesting ones before tossing them into the fields they walked past. He picked up a stick and pretended it was a sword. "I'm a powerful knight." He thrust the sword in front of him, sidestepping an invisible opponent, then parried and made a slicing motion. "Gotcha!" he shouted.

Cooper heard him, turned around and grinned, and then returned his attention to the oxen.

Tim tucked his stick-sword into the waist of his pants. "I sure like Mr. Jerome. Don't you, Ma?"

Hallie peered down at her son. "I surely do."

Tim observed, "Sometimes I think he's sad, though. You know, maybe if he talked about it, he would feel better. Like whenever I talk to you about losin' Pa, I feel better." He paused and then lifted his head to stare into his mother's eyes. "Do you think we should tell him he might feel better if he talked about what's makin' him sad?"

Hallie closed her gaping mouth. How should she answer her son's wisdom? "Tim, sometimes it's best to let a person come to that conclusion on his own. I don't think Mr. Jerome is ready to talk about whatever it is."

They walked on in silence for several minutes and then Tim said, "Okay, Ma, I won't say anything, but I sure hope Mr. Jerome figures it out, 'cause it might make him happier."

Later, when the wagons in front of them slowed to a crawl, Hallie craned her neck to see what lay ahead. The wagons halted and Cooper said, "We're coming to a junction. We're backed up because some of the trains ahead of ours are turning west to follow the Santa Fe Trail into New Mexico Territory, but others, like us, are continuing northwest. After we pass the junction, our speed will pick up again, but we won't get far before it's time to make camp."

That night as they lay inside their wagon, Tim snoring contentedly, Hallie reached to move the flap aside and contemplate the stars. A smile lifted the corners of her mouth as she whispered, "Thank you, Lord, for sending Cooper to guide us on this long journey."

Chapter 12: Caress

After four days travel from Westport the captain's warning about over packing could be seen in the belongings previous trains had pitched to the side of the road. Even some folks in their own train had to lighten their loads.

They also established a daily routine. Rising at daylight, fires were lit, bodies were washed and dressed, men and older children tended to the animals, and women and younger children prepared the morning meal. Throughout the morning ritual, Captain Jones and his leaders circled the wagons on horseback looking for potential mechanical problems, seeing how folks were faring, and offering encouragement.

Hallie couldn't help but notice that the leaders spent the least amount of time with the Pittance group. Although Cooper didn't avoid them, his temperament after a visit was always dark. Hallie could only imagine Mrs. Pittance's distasteful behavior. Pastor Pittance, big-boned, gray-eyed, with a long white beard the same color as his close-cropped hair, was less vocal than his wife. In fact, he seemed content to observe and not interfere with his congregation—very peculiar to Hallie's way of thinking. Her own pastor in Jebson had overseen his flock like a mother bear protecting her cubs, and the parishioners were loving country folk who did everything in their power to help each other and strangers. Yes, the Pittance group was strange, indeed.

As for Tim, he was always captivated by birds, small creatures scurrying in the underbrush, the occasional snake or other reptile, and even the changing flora and scenery. He truly had inherited his father's love of knowledge and heart for adventure.

The most difficult aspect of the journey for Hallie was the continuous walking, of which Cooper was mindful. Often, he turned around with an expression that said as loud as words: *It's time to climb in the wagon.* Halting the oxen, he would then help her onto the wagon seat where she would ride for the next hour, sometimes even longer.

On the day of their scheduled arrival at the Wakarusa river crossing, Hallie was happily observing nature with Tim and sharing her excitement of reaching a milestone when she stumbled over a protruding tree root. Sharp pain shot up her ankle and she gasped, falling to her knees.

Tim yelled, "Mr. Jerome! Ma's hurt!"

Immediately Cooper jerked around, halted the oxen, and rushed to help.

When the blackness that accompanied near fainting subsided, Hallie tried to make light of her injury. "Dumb me. I wasn't looking where I was going." She attempted to rise, but excruciating pain caused her to groan and drop back down.

Cooper ordered, "Don't move. Tim, run ahead and let Captain Jones know what's happened."

Hallie said, "I'm so sorry. Now I've held the train up and we were almost to the river. I feel terrible."

"These things happen, dear."

Cooper's endearment clutched Hallie's heart and made it flutter. For a second, her pain was forgotten.

He continued, "I need to determine if your ankle is broken before moving you."

Numbly, she nodded.

Cooper lifted her skirt to uncover her ankle and gently probed it through the leather of her shoe. Hallie couldn't take her eyes off his fingers testing her mobility. He looked up and smiled encouragingly. "I don't think it's broken. Your high top shoe probably kept that from happening."

Hallie nodded again, her pain falling low on her list of priorities as long as Cooper's eyes, the same color as the cloudless sky, held her gaze.

He said gently, "Put your arms around my neck so I can lift you into the wagon."

When he bent and placed one arm under her back and the other under her legs, she encircled his neck and had an almost overwhelming desire to snuggle her head against his broad chest.

Several of their fellow travelers rushed to assist and Captain Jones galloped over on Midnight, his powerful black gelding. In his booming voice he ordered the pioneers to step aside and reached Hallie just as Cooper lifted her into the back of the wagon.

Cooper said, "She's got a bad sprain. But I'd appreciate your opinion."

Captain Jones dismounted and Cooper backed away. The gentle probing of the Captain's big hands belied his rough personage and he smiled encouragingly. "I think you're right, Cooper, it's a sprain, but let's get the shoe off and recheck it before it swells more."

Cooper glanced at Hallie. "This is going to hurt, so it's okay if you need to yell."

Hallie nodded her understanding and clasped her hands tightly together while Cooper slowly unlaced and removed her shoe. Pain shot to the top of her head, but she refused to vocalize her discomfort or appear feeble in the eyes of the crowd now gathered at the back of her wagon. She was unable to stifle a moan, however.

Once her shoe was off, another examination confirmed no broken bones and the pioneers released a corporate sigh of relief. Captain Jones ordered everyone back to their wagons and mounted Midnight. To Cooper, he said, "Send the boy to the front to let me know when you're ready to move on."

Cooper responded, "Yes, sir; should be about a quarter hour."

Tim hovered close to the wagon, worried. "You feelin' better, Ma?"

Wanting to comfort and reassure him, although her ankle throbbed, she said, "I am, son. Don't you worry about me; I'll be right as rain in a couple of days."

Her answer brightened his expression. Cooper suggested, "We need to cool and wrap your ma's ankle. Why don't you climb in the wagon and hand me those strips of cloth we got stored and then wet a towel."

"Yes, sir."

Tim circled the wagon, hoisted himself through the front, and opened the leather satchel stocked with medical supplies. After digging in the bag, he handed the cloth strips to Cooper who set them aside temporarily. Cooper turned his gaze on Hallie and asked, "Do you want some laudanum?"

Hallie had no intention of taking the powerful drug that would only make her sleep. "No, I don't think so. I want to stay awake."

The wagon jostled when Tim jumped down to the ground. He opened the lid of the water barrel fastened to the frame and then walked to the back to hand Cooper a wet towel.

Hallie watched Cooper gently place the cool cloth on her ankle, the ministration of his hands stealing her breath. She felt like a fireball on the verge of exploding. When his fingers left the cloth and stroked her calf beneath her skirt in an intimate caress, God help her, she didn't want him to stop.

* * *

Cooper jerked his hand from Hallie's leg and swore under his breath. *My God, have you lost your mind?*

Seeing Hallie's widened eyes, he knew she had not misunderstood his caress. Glancing away, he said matter-of-factly, "Looks like you'll be down for a few days, but that'll give your feet time to heal from the blisters." He directed his words to Tim who was placing the lid back on the water barrel. "Tim, guess you'll be doing a few extra chores for awhile, but I know you can handle it."

Tim replied seriously, "Yes, sir. Whatever you and ma need."

Cooper glanced back at Hallie. "I need to wrap your ankle so we can get this train moving again."

Hallie met his gaze and quickly darted her eyes to her skirt, playing with a fold. "That's okay; I can do it."

Hell. Now I've got her avoiding me. "Alright."

For the next two hours, Cooper berated himself for giving in to his desire to caress Hallie. When the noon break was called, he hurried to check on her. She had wrapped her ankle tightly, but she was still avoiding his gaze. Somehow he had to get them back on familiar footing.

Cooper sent Tim to gather firewood because he needed privacy with Hallie to apologize, and hopefully, get them back on track. After Tim left, he asked, "How are you feeling?"

"It's bearable," she said in a small voice, gazing at the top of the canvas.

Gathering his courage, Cooper said, "Hallie, please look at me."

He watched the swallowing motion of her throat and his stomach knotted, but he continued anyway. "I want you to understand something."

She turned green eyes on him and nodded almost imperceptibly.

"First, I want to apologize for my behavior earlier." When she didn't respond, he continued, "You know what I'm talking about, don't you?"

She nodded slightly again.

"I…" He found it almost impossible to continue. He tried again. "I haven't enjoyed a woman's company for a long time and touching a woman is…pleasurable." *God, Cooper, you sound like an ass.* "What I'm trying to say is, I'm sorry, and it won't happen again. You hired me to do a job and I intend to get you and Tim to Oregon and settled. I don't want you to be afraid of me or avoid me. What happened…won't happen again. Can we go back to the way things were?"

* * *

Two emotions bombarded Hallie: relief and disappointment. Relief for obvious reasons, but her disappointment distressed her. According to Cooper's confession, his reaction would have been the same with any woman, and that was disappointing.

Sure, she understood that a man had lustful desires at times. Even her soft-spoken, kindly Thomas, had occasionally been overcome by it, and she had enjoyed that part of their lives, but never had she experienced the all consuming fire ignited by Cooper's breathtakingly sensual touch.

Chapter 13: Crossing the Wakarusa

Tim ran to the back of the wagon and peeked his head inside. "Ma, we've reached the Wakarusa."

"Goodness, let me look out the front." It had been two hours since lunch and Hallie hobbled to the front of the wagon to gaze at what appeared to be a gently flowing river, and her anxiety eased.

Walking beside the oxen, Cooper called "Gee," and cracked his whip in the air. Seeing Hallie peek out, he smiled and she warmly returned his smile, forgetting for the moment her awkward feelings in the face of this new adventure.

Cooper motioned ahead. "We'll follow the river a short ways and then arrive at Blue Jacket's Ferry. We might get some of the wagons crossed today, but probably not all."

Hallie said, "I had visions of a rushing river, not this slow moving one."

"Don't let this river fool you; it's more dangerous than it looks." He pointed to the banks. "In the early days of the trail, wagons had to be dismantled and lowered down those limestone banks with ropes before being towed across and then roped up on the other side."

"Oh, those poor people; thank goodness we have a ferry."

The wagons in front of them came to a halt and Cooper called, "Whoa!"

Captain Jones trotted his horse the length of the train, instructing everyone to secure their belongings.

With Tim's help, Hallie made sure everything was firmly fastened inside their wagon, while Cooper took care of the outside. After that, she sat on the wagon seat and gingerly tried to find a comfortable position for her ankle while waiting their turn. If there was one thing she had discovered since beginning her journey, it was that everything moved at a snail's pace.

An hour later, they had advanced to the front of the line and Hallie breathed a sigh of relief. Soon they would be on the other side. She watched Cooper speaking with the Indians operating the ferry and was surprised when he came back and said, "This ferry is smaller than I expected so I'm not taking any chances. Even though it will cost two ferry tolls, we're splitting our animals up to cross over. If something happens, it's better to lose some of them, and not all."

Hallie considered his words and decided it was a wise decision. She watched him unhitch two of the oxen and then load them, along with the extra ox and milk cow, onto the ferry.

Behind them, one of the pioneers yelled, "You're just making this crossing that much longer! Nothing happened to the wagons and animals ahead of you!"

Cooper didn't give a look or offer an explanation to the offended man. The man continued to grumble loudly and voice his opinion to Captain Jones when he rode past.

Captain Jones halted Midnight and responded, "Now, Mr. Liverman, of course you're entitled to your opinion, and believe me, we've all heard it, but that's not going to change Cooper's decision. So I suggest you quit your belly achin' and just wait your turn. I'll not interfere with a man who's being rightfully cautious."

Leaning from her perch, Hallie watched Mr. Liverman narrow his eyes at the captain and open his mouth to reply, but Mrs. Liverman elbowed him and said something under her breath. After that he stomped to the back of his wagon.

Shifting her attention to the ferry, she watched it transport her animals to the other side and return. Cooper now guided the remaining oxen as they pulled the wagon aboard the ferry and then he loaded Sweet Pea. Tim sat on the wagon seat alongside Hallie and she bit her bottom lip as the ferry was pulled across the river. Standing behind the wagon, Cooper held the reins of Sweet Pea. As smooth as could be expected, the ferry docked on the other side.

Before long, the animals and wagon were unloaded and the ferry was on its way back across the Wakarusa. Cooper tied Sweet Pea to the back of the wagon and guided the oxen in pulling the schooner farther up the bank to join the other oxen and cow. While he attended to the animals, Hallie moved to the rear of the wagon to watch the continued crossings of the other emigrants. Mr. Liverman had crowded all of his animals and family onto the ferry, and he had more animals than Hallie.

"Please let them make it over safely," Hallie whispered a quiet prayer. Having just crossed the river, she understood the fear written on Mrs. Liverman's face.

About three-quarters of the way across, a horse spooked and reared on its hind legs, and even though one of the Liverman boys tried to hold the reins and calm the beast, it lunged for the river. Mr. Liverman tried to edge around his other animals, but he didn't make it in time. Mrs. Liverman screamed when both the horse and her son plunged into the river.

Horrified, Hallie watched Mr. Liverman dive in after his son. The horse swam toward shore and the Liverman boy went underwater. His mother yelled, "He's afraid of the water. He can't swim!"

Suddenly, Hallie saw Cooper running toward the river. He pulled off his boots and dived in, his powerful strokes pulling him in the direction the boy had disappeared. Mr. Liverman reached the spot before Cooper and disappeared under water, too. After a minute he reappeared, but his son did not. Mrs. Liverman started screaming, "Find my boy! Find my boy! He's only twelve!"

Cooper took a deep breath before diving under. Praying fiercely, Hallie whispered over and over, "Save him…save him.." Clasping her hands over her heart, sweat beaded on her forehead and her heart pounded.

Time seemed to stand still while Cooper and Mr. Liverman swam under water searching for the boy. Hallie went from breathing rapidly to holding her breath. And just when it seemed the suspense would never end, Cooper jerked the boy out of the water and Mr. Liverman's head popped up at the same time. Together, they hauled the boy to the bank and other men ran to help haul him up the limestone rocks. The ferry banked and Mrs. Liverman grabbed up her skirts and rushed to disembark while her older children and the Indian operator hurried to unload the ferry.

Ignoring the pain in her ankle, Hallie lowered herself to the ground, instructed Tim to stay with their wagon, and hobbled to the lifeless boy. Cooper clambered up the rocks and turned the child onto his side, attempting to express water from his lungs. After several maneuvers the boy suddenly coughed up water and dragged a ragged breath. Hallie and Mrs. Liverman, on their knees beside the child, exclaimed their relief. After a few more minutes, Cooper stepped aside and left the boy to the attention of his parents.

Hallie called for Tim to bring towels and then painfully started toward her wagon. Suddenly, wet arms lifted her and she squealed.

Cooper said low, "Hallie, I sure hope you haven't reinjured your ankle."

The rest of the day proceeded with no more mishaps. Captain Jones instructed the pioneers who had crossed over to continue on for a mile before breaking for camp and to wait for him and the other pioneers before continuing the next day.

That night, with half the camp circled, Hallie sat comfortably in her chair with her leg propped on a bucket and listened to Cooper and Tim try to outdo each other in ghost stories. She smiled when Tim related one of the stories he had often begged his father to tell on long winter nights before a blazing fire. Just when he got to the scary part, Mr. Liverman stepped into the firelight and startled her.

Cooper said, "Hello, Mr. Liverman. How's Peter feeling?"

Mr. Liverman cleared his throat. "He's doing right fine—thanks to you."

No one said anything and the stocky man continued. "I just came to apologize for my behavior this afternoon. If I'd followed your lead..." his voice cracked, "my boy wouldn't have gone through this." He spread his hands wide. "I just want you to know how sorry I am, and if you need *anything,* you just let me know."

Cooper rose and extended his hand. "Thank you, Mr. Liverman. Everyone does things they wish they could change. If I were to repeat my own list..." he smiled, "it would be a long one."

Mr. Liverman said, "You're being kind when I deserve a punch in the mouth." He gave a little laugh. "Please call me Hank."

Cooper said, "And you must call me Cooper."

After that, Hank related to Cooper some mechanical problems he was having with his wagon and asked for advice. While they talked and Tim stoked the fire, Hallie closed her eyes and replayed Cooper's response to Mr. Liverman's apology. He had been kind and forgiving, even gentle, when he could have thrown the apology back in the poor man's face and spoken as harshly as Mr. Liverman had that afternoon. *You're a wise man, Cooper.*

Chapter 14: Carvings at Alcove Spring

Ten days and three river crossings later—the lower Kansas and the Little and Big Vermillions—the wagons circled at Alcove Spring. Captain Jones had said it was a popular location and Hallie could see by the ruts of previous wagons over many years that it was so.

With her ankle almost healed, she now walked a good portion of each day, and her blisters were gone. Cooper was polite and aloof and she knew he was trying to make her feel comfortable around him.

Gazing over the terrain, she exclaimed to Tim and Cooper, "It's simply beautiful here. If Oregon is half this pretty, I shall be forever happy."

After setting up camp, Cooper told Hallie and Tim, "I've been checking out the spring. Come see the names of pioneers carved into the rocks."

Happy to have something to do other than the usual routine, Hallie and Tim followed Cooper to a stream with water cascading over a ledge that jutted about twelve feet above a basin.

Tim bent to splash the water in the basin and exclaimed, "It's so cold!"

Hallie tried it for herself. "Oh, it is!"

Then Cooper pointed to carvings on the ledge.

For the next few minutes, they read the names and dates of pioneers as far back as the 1840s. Hallie was pensive. "Just think, all these people have paved the Westward Trails for us." She touched one of the names. "And now, we're paving the way for those after us."

Cooper asked, "Would you like for me to carve your names?"

Hallie met his gaze and in that moment felt a spiritual bond not only with Cooper, but with the thousands who had blazed this trail, sometimes with laughter, often with tears. Carving their own names into the ledge would forever join them with those brave souls exemplifying the courage of the human spirit to chase dreams, no matter how elusive or difficult.

"Yes," she breathed.

Cooper removed the knife sheathed to his thigh and cocked his head toward Tim. "Where would you like your name, son?

Perhaps not understanding the magnitude of the moment, but seeing the tears brimming in his mother's eyes, Tim stepped to a stone and pointed. "There, sir."

After Cooper had carved Tim's name he asked Hallie, "Where would you like your name?"

"Below Tim's. And, Cooper, you must also carve your name."

Perched next to her son, Hallie watched her name being etched into history. Tim whispered, "Ma, someday I'll return and find our names."

Hallie patted his hand and tried to memorialize the magic of the waterfall, the stream, the rocks, the foliage, the sky, and Tim and Cooper in her mind and emotions.

Cooper turned, wiped his blade on his pants, and then sheathed it. "We've left our marks." He stared at Hallie.

Late that evening, while Hallie sat and watched the fires burning around the circle of wagons and listened to the sounds of camp—horses neighing, a mother calling her child, fires crackling, a man's laugh—she contemplated her day and allowed the peaceful night to seep into her soul, refusing to worry about the future or the chores to be done on the morrow.

"Excuse me, Miz Wells. Could I talk to you a minute?" Hallie was surprised to see one of the fancy women approaching.

"Of course, please sit." Hallie motioned to the chair Cooper had vacated to go in search of Captain Jones.

"Thank you, ma'am." The pretty redhead now wearing a dress more suitable to their journey, but still so tight in the bodice as to push the swell of her breasts over the top of the rounded neckline, daintily sat on the chair.

Seeing the woman up close, Hallie was surprised by how beautiful she was, and young. The girl looked to be no more than eighteen or twenty, with exquisite coloring, absent the freckles that so often accompanied red hair. Even by firelight, her clear blue eyes in a delicate face held the freshness of innocence, startling when one considered her occupation.

The girl fidgeted and said, "My name is Clarissa and I…well…got elected by the other ladies in our group to ask you something."

Hallie furrowed her brow. "What can I do for you, Clarissa?"

"Well, me and the other ladies…well, we like you, and we seen how that preacher woman treats you—she treats us the same. Anyway, 'cause we like you so much we wanted to ask you first."

The woman studied her nails and Hallie prompted, "What do you want to ask me?"

Clarissa leaned forward and said low, "We wanted to know if you have feelins' for Mr. Jerome, 'cause if you do...we won't pursue him. We may be fancy women, but we got morals, and if you want him to be your man, we won't do anything. But if you don't..." Clarissa grinned, "we'd sure like to spend time with him...if you get my meanin'." She winked.

Hallie's eyes widened and then her mouth fell open. Clarissa waited for her response.

Hallie stuttered, "Uh...uh...no...no...I don't have feelings for Mr. Jerome."

Clarissa grinned and clapped her hands. "The ladies are gonna be so happy 'bout that!" She leaned closer. "We just think he's the handsomest man ever, and so nice and respectful of the ladies." She leaned even closer and whispered, "I'd just *love* to marry a man like him."

Before Hallie could respond, Clarissa jumped up. "I gotta go tell the ladies. We wasn't sure how you felt 'bout him 'cause sometimes we seen you starin' at him, but now that you said it's okay, we're gonna make him *real* happy. Thank you, Miz Wells." She started to turn around, but paused. "Is it okay if we call you Hallie?"

"Yes, of course."

Clarissa grinned, made a little waving motion, and skipped back to her wagon.

"Was that one of the women from Mrs. Martinique's group?"

Hallie jumped at the sound of Cooper's voice when he stepped into the firelight.

"Uh...yes."

"What did she want?"

"She…uh…she…"

Cooper waited.

"She just wanted to introduce herself. She said she and the ladies didn't like the way Mrs. Pittance had treated me." Hallie jumped up. "I…I need to check on Tim. He's with the Livermans." She rushed away from her wagon.

The next morning, Tim said, "Ma, Cooper said we're gonna cross the Big Blue today at Independence Crossing. I think crossing rivers is my favorite part of the trail. I can't wait to do it again."

Although crossing rivers was Hallie's least favorite and tied her stomach in knots, she smiled at her son's enthusiasm.

Before noon, they reached Independence Crossing and the large ferry, so different from the previous ones, helped relieve her mind. Cooper seemed to understand, saying, "We won't have to split up the animals this time."

By evening all of the emigrants under Captain Jones's care had been ferried across with nary an incident. At dusk, they joyously camped on the other side of the river, having notched another crossing on their belts. Taking advantage of abundant water, women washed their babies and small children in barrels, while older children splashed in the shallows and some even swam in the depths. Hallie followed Tim to the river's edge and laughed as he and Sam played with newfound friends. She decided that later she would return and bathe when everyone was gone.

After lying in bed and waiting for camp to settle, Hallie slipped out the back of her wagon with a towel and a special bar of soap Thomas had given her. She had already unbound her hair and tied the mass back with a ribbon. She could smell the river and anticipated bathing with excitement, missing the elaborate tub Thomas had bought her and his teasing about prune skin.

Now, reaching the river, she glanced around to make sure she was alone before setting her towel on the ground, slipping the soap from her pocket, and letting her cloak fall to the ground. Still wearing her shift, she stepped to the water's edge and then waded to her knees; she had no intention of undressing. Enjoying the balmy breeze, she pulled the ribbon from her hair and bent forward to dip her long mane in the water. Before long, her hair was lathered and she bent again to rinse it. Oh, the pleasure of fresh water and cleanliness; washing from a basin was nothing compared to this.

* * *

Cooper watched Hallie in the moonlight and held his breath. Her uplifted face radiated ecstasy. Her fluid movements and the look on her face made him want to wade into the water, take her in his arms, and taste every part of her body. She was the most graceful woman he had ever encountered. His penchant for large, buxom women rushed out the door as he watched this gazelle. He grinned when he imagined the embarrassment that would rosy her cheeks and body if she knew he was watching.

The shift Hallie was wearing slipped from her shoulder revealing a small, pale breast. Cooper whooshed and knew he should look away, but he couldn't make himself do so. He wanted the whole

112

damn gown to fall to the ground. He almost groaned aloud when she righted the sleeve and slipped back into her cloak. With a glorious mane of hair hanging to her waist, she walked back to camp and Cooper followed.

Chapter 15: Bad Dream at Fremont Springs

Five days later they reached Fremont Springs and camped. With nowhere to afford privacy, Hallie washed herself with a cloth alongside the other women at the spring.

Late that night something startled her awake. Lifting on her elbow, she pulled aside the canvas, allowing enough moonlight inside to see Tim's face. Sometimes he had bad dreams about his father's death, but the shaft of light showed him sleeping peacefully.

Lying back down and folding her hands under her cheek, she had just closed her eyes when she heard a moan. Faster than a deer trying to escape a mountain lion her heart galloped. The sound was coming from just outside her wagon where Cooper slept. *Is Cooper hurt?*

Rising swiftly but quietly to her knees, she peered around the canvas. A three-quarter moon bathed the camp in silvery light and Hallie's eyes adjusted quickly. Cooper lay in his bedroll a few feet away, tossing like he was having a nightmare and making another pitiful sound.

Disregarding her bare feet and nightgown she let herself to the ground and tiptoed toward Cooper. From his expression she could see that he was in the throes of a bad dream, and could only imagine the torment that would cause such twisted features.

Softly kneeling beside him, she touched his shoulder. "Cooper, wake up; you're dreaming."

Cooper moved so fast Hallie didn't have time to be terrified. One minute she was on her feet, the next she was flat on her back in the dust with his hands around her neck. She just stared up at him with saucer eyes.

"Damn!" He jumped backward and jerked his hands above his head, whispering angrily, "What the hell are you doing, Hallie?"

"You...you were having a nightmare and I was trying to wake you."

"Dammit, woman, don't you know that sneaking up on a man can get you killed?"

The tone of his voice and the fact that he was talking to her like a child again bristled the hair on her arms and removed any trepidation.

Still lying on the ground, she whispered just as adamantly, "Mr. Jerome, you were moaning like an injured animal and I considered it an act of charitable kindness to wake you. However, if you prefer your nightmares, please step aside and allow me to return to my wagon!" Having had her say, she pushed into a seated position and started to rise. Cooper sat in the dirt and brought his legs up to his chest, wrapping his arms around them and placing his forehead on his knees.

In a muffled and contrite voice he said, "My apologies, ma'am. You're right about me having a nightmare and no, I don't like having them. Thank you for trying to help. I learned my reflexes in the army. Sometimes reflexes were all that stood between me and death."

The sadness in Cooper's voice removed any hostility Hallie was feeling and she lowered herself back to the ground. "Were you dreaming about the war?"

"Yes, ma'am."

Inhaling a long, slow breath, Hallie reached her hand toward one of his and touched her finger to it. "Do you want to talk about it?"

She moved her hand until she could hold his, not expecting him to return her grasp. When he did, she almost moved her other hand to stroke his hair. Because such an act would be too foreword, she forced her hand to stay at her side and waited for whatever would happen next.

After a lengthy silence, Cooper turned his head so that his cheek rested on his knees and spoke quietly. "I killed my fair share of men in the war. Course it was either kill or be killed, but that still don't stop the dreams. I think about the families of those men, some so young as to almost still be boys, and I want to throw my guts up knowing the heartache I've caused some mother and father."

Hallie squeezed her eyes at the pain in Cooper's voice. Disregarding her previous restraint, she lifted her free hand to his black hair, now free of its leather restraint and falling forward, and combed her fingers through its silky, charcoal thickness. She wanted to caress his cheek. Instead, she said, "Someday you'll come to terms with what happened, but until then, I want you to know that I consider you to be a good and just man. I know that you would not frivolously take the life of another. And the fact that you have nightmares

116

about it only proves the goodness of your heart." She felt Cooper tighten his hold on her hand and she continued. "If the tables were turned and you were the dead soldier, what would you say to the man who had taken your life? Would you hold it against him for fighting in a battle and killing you?"

For a long time, they sat facing each other with their hands locked and Hallie stroking Cooper's hair. Finally, he let go of her hand and lifted his head. "Goodnight, Hallie." In the moonlight the planes of his face appeared hewn from stone.

Hallie removed her hand from his hair and whispered, "Goodnight, Cooper."

Chapter 16: Narrow Escape at The Narrows

A few days after Cooper's nightmare, the emigrants reached an area called The Narrows. With a bluff on one side and the Little Blue River on the other, the wagons had to travel single file. Cooper said they were almost two hundred and fifty miles out of Westport. The fact that they had only traversed an eighth of their journey boggled Hallie's mind. She already felt as if she were thousands of miles from Jebson.

Since the night she attempted to comfort Cooper after his nightmare, he had been cordial and always seemed to find chores keeping him on the outskirts of their wagon when they camped. Hallie worried that she had been too forward in touching him. The thought that perhaps he wasn't thinking well of her any longer, saddened her.

Turning her attention back to their narrow path, she shrieked, "Tim, stop! Don't move an inch!"

Tim halted and looked questioningly up at his mother.

Gingerly, she said, "There's a rattlesnake right in front of us."

Tim's eyes widened and his mouth formed an "O."

The sudden crack of gunfire startled them both and Hallie screamed. Cooper holstered his gun. "Sorry to scare you, but I wasn't taking any chances."

The sound of the shot brought people running to their wagon, even Stubby and Harley, but when Cooper glanced up and saw them, his scowl sent them backtracking fast.

Captain Jones galloped up. "Yep. I thought the problem was a snake. Like I explained last night, this place is famous for them."

To Hallie's horror, Captain Jones dismounted and scooped the snake up by its tail. "This is going to make a fine dinner; some of the best meat around is rattlesnake. Mind if I share it with ya'll?"

Cooper looked at Hallie and grinned. "Ah, Captain, you go ahead and enjoy it. I think we'll pass."

Captain Jones shrugged. "Okay, but you don't know what you're missin'. After I eat the meat, the skin is goin' to make a fine band for my hat and the rattle's a dandy decoration."

After the captain trotted away on Midnight, Hallie shuddered and Cooper laughed. Tim, always curious, asked, "Ma, do you think I could taste some of that rattlesnake meat after Captain Jones gets it cooked?"

Hallie stared at her son with incredulity. "No."

That night, after passing through The Narrows, and some of the other emigrants also having close calls with rattlers, Captain Jones approached their wagon on foot. He said, "I was feelin' right guilty 'bout takin' yer snake, so I brought the skin and rattles back for Tim. They'll be souvenirs from his travels." He stuck out the hand that had been hidden behind his back and dangled the snakeskin toward Tim. The rattles rested in his palm.

Tim jumped up. "Wow! That's great!" He looked at his mother with pleading eyes. "Can I have them? Please, Ma."

Hallie glanced at Cooper and could almost hear his thought. *The boy's havin' to grow up fast. Don't deny him.*

Hallie nodded. "Sure, Tim. They'll be great reminders of our journey; one we'll talk about on cold winters before a fire."

As if the snakeskin and rattles were precious jewels, Tim accepted them from Captain Jones.

The captain said, "Now the skin still needs to dry, so find a place to hang it."

"Yes, sir. I got just the place."

* * *

Cooper grinned thinking about Hallie's shocked expression when Captain Jones brought the snakeskin to their camp earlier. He was proud of her allowing Tim to keep it, although she loathed the thing. For all of her motherly instincts, he could see she was trying to let her son mature.

Taking another drag of his rolled cigarette, he inhaled and closed his eyes, envisioning Hallie beside the river with her hair hanging loose and her gown slipped.

"Good evening, Mr. Jerome," said a throaty voice.

Cooper opened his eyes to see one of the fancy ladies approaching. It was the redhead; the one who was a real looker; the one who turned men's heads and ignited resentment in their wives.

"Good evening—Miz Wickens, isn't it?"

"Yes, but please call me Clarissa."

"It's nice to make your acquaintance."

"Likewise, sir."

Clarissa straightened her shoulders, which pushed the large swell of her bosom forward. But rather than entice Cooper, it amused him. The girl was probably barely out of her teens. She stepped closer and lifted a hand to finger his collar. "Me and the other gals have had our eyes on you."

He smiled and played her game. "Is that right?"

"Yep. That's right. In fact, we had a fight about which one of us could approach you first." She lifted the finger on his collar to the stubble on his face. "But they finally let me 'cause I'm the youngest."

Cooper repeated, "Is that right?"

"Yep. So…how do you think I should be rewarded?"

To say Cooper wasn't having fun would be a lie—he hadn't flirted in a long time—so he kept the conversation going. "How do you want to be rewarded?"

Clarissa pouted, pursed her lips, and finally sucked her bottom lip into her mouth. "Maybe we could start with a kiss."

Before Cooper knew what she was about, her mouth was jammed against his and he couldn't decide whether to give in to the kiss or push her away. Just when he'd decided to push her away, a rustling distracted them. Placing his hands on Clarissa shoulders and setting her backward, he looked past her to see Hallie with her mouth agape.

Oh, hell!

Clarissa turned to see Hallie and laughed. "It's okay Cooper; Hallie's already given her permission."

"Huh?"

"We wanted to make sure Hallie didn't have dibs on you, so we asked, and she said she didn't."

Confused, Cooper stared at Hallie, who made a choking sound, whirled, and fled back in the direction of her wagon.

Clarissa asked, "Did I say something wrong? Is there something between you two?"

"No. Nothing."

The strumpet grinned and giggled. "Great. Do you want to find some place private to get acquainted?"

Cooper watched Hallie's retreating back. "Um, I'm kind of tired; maybe another time." Before Clarissa could respond, he stomped back to camp.

* * *

Hallie couldn't inhale enough air and her heart beat so fast she was sure she wouldn't make it back to her wagon without fainting. She'd only fainted once, giving birth to Tim when the pain had become unbearable. Other than that, she'd endured the death of loved ones and physical work to the point of collapse, and never fainted. But seeing Cooper with the beautiful Clarissa affected her more than she could have imagined possible.

Hastening her steps, she finally reached her wagon and lifted the flap, wanting to thank the stars that Tim was asleep. Slipping into her wagon, she berated herself for being captured by the beauty of the moon and walking farther from camp than she intended. She pulled her legs to her chest and rested her head on her knees.

Breathe slow…breathe slow.

She just got her breathing under control when Cooper's voice called softly outside her wagon. "Hallie. Can I have a minute of your time?"

Her heart slammed her ribs in a rapid staccato and her breathing became little pants.

"Hallie?" he repeated.

Clearing her throat, she said. "I-I'm already in bed. Maybe we could talk later."

There was a pause before Cooper responded, "No. ma'am, it can't wait until later. I'll wait for you by the oxen."

Before she could refuse, she heard Cooper's retreating footsteps.

Damn. Shocked at herself for thinking a curse word, when she had always prided herself for avoiding the use of vulgarity, she inhaled a gulp of air and slowly edged toward the canvas flap. Inhaling once more, she lowered herself to the ground and walked toward the animals.

Face it; you're afraid Cooper is attracted to Clarissa. Hallie answered her own thought. *Well, his attraction is obvious. He was kissing her.* Hallie's mind kept up its conversation. *But why should you care? As long as he does his job and gets you and Tim to Oregon, what he does on his own time is his business.* She saw his dark figure and gulped. *Then why does it hurt so bad?*

Cooper advanced toward her and she stopped, waiting for his approach. Hopefully, there was no one close enough to hear their conversation. He halted inches from her and came right to the point. "What you saw wasn't what it appeared to be."

Hallie's voice sounded breathless when she responded, "You don't have to explain–"

"Yes, I do. I am not the kind of man who chases fancy women while traveling on a wagon train. The woman…well…she initiated the kiss and I was just about to stop it when you saw us."

Relief flooded Hallie, which made her angry at herself. She was newly widowed; she shouldn't care about Cooper's romantic encounters. She didn't know how to respond, so she said, "Thank you for making that clear. Good night, Cooper." She started to turn away.

"Not so fast, Hallie."

Pausing, she felt herself trembling at the deepness of his voice. Lifting her gaze to his, with the moonlight turning the color and intensity of his eyes to that of a churning sea, she waited for the question she knew was coming.

"What did Clarissa mean when she said you gave the gals permission?"

Lowering her lashes, Hallie wished the ground would open and swallow her up. "Ah … well … she … they … wanted to know if you and I … ah … you know … because they thought you … ah … were handsome … and didn't want ..." She lifted her hand to finger a tear. She sounded like a brainless idiot.

Quietly, Cooper said, "You don't have to say any more. I get the picture. But just so you understand, I'm not interested in pleasuring myself with any of them. Go back to bed, Hallie."

* * *

Cooper watched Hallie's swiftly retreating back and ground his jaw. The only one he wanted to pleasure himself with was her. *Damn!*

Chapter 17: The Lone Tree

The pioneers now traveled through rolling hills covered with grasses and nary a tree in sight. Beyond the hills, far in the distance, steep mountains rose in majestic beauty. To avoid the ruts of wagons gone before them, as well as the ruts of their own wagons, the prairie schooners traveled several abreast, like a small herd of animals migrating westward following their lead beast, Captain Jones. Hallie chuckled at the vision in her mind.

As if conjuring Captain Jones up, he cantered Midnight to their wagon. "Howdy, Cooper, Miz Wells, Tim."

"Good morning, Captain. It's a beautiful day," Hallie responded.

"That it is. I always enjoy this part of the journey. The travelin's easy and the scenery spectacular."

Cooper said, "We should reach Fort Kearney in a couple of days. Don't you think?"

"Yep. Once we get there, we'll regroup, check supplies, and then head out after a day or so." Captain Jones glanced at Tim. "I'm gonna ride around the train; check things out. Would you like to hop on the back of Midnight and come along? Two eyes are better 'n one."

Tim shouted, "That'd be great!"

Captain Jones looked slightly embarrassed. "Er, I guess I should'a asked yer ma if it was okay first."

Tim turned pleading eyes on his mother. Hallie laughed. "It's perfectly fine. Tim was getting bored anyway."

Tim grinned as Captain Jones reached down to haul him up behind him. Before he nudged his horse away, the captain scowled and pointed in the distance. His voice sounded both sad and angry. "There used to be a lone tree over that-a-way. It was a trail marker we even called The Lone Tree. Just imagine, in this vast grassland, that single tree withstood the elements for probably hundreds of years...but it sure couldn't withstand man. It was like a sentinel suddenly chopped down; literally." He shook his head. "It happened back in the late forties." He shook his head again. "The insensitivity of people boggles the mind."

After the captain and Tim galloped away, Hallie tried to concentrate on the beauty around her, but her gaze kept being drawn to Cooper's broad back. Since finding him with Clarissa and his subsequent explanation of the kiss she'd seen, and then her own admission of Clarissa's visit to ask permission to pursue him, she had avoided him. Having Tim around had helped in that endeavor. Now it was just the two of them walking the grassland with the closest wagon shouting distance away.

Hallie wished things could go back to the way they were in Westport when they had talked about supplies and concentrated on preparing for the journey. She focused on distant mountain peaks for a short time before returning her gaze to Cooper. He moved with an easy grace, but was as rugged as the terrain they trod upon. And, like the mountains ahead of them, there was much to be discovered. God help her, she wanted to know his secrets. She wanted to know what caused the sadness in his eyes. Was it more than just the war? Thomas, her beloved husband, had always been an open book. He had spoken freely of his feelings, dreams, aspirations, and he'd encouraged her to speak freely of hers. Their relationship had always been an easy one. He never tied her stomach in knots or made her wax hot and cold just by being in his presence.

Hallie's thoughts took an unexpected turn. Because she had never been with any man—in the biblical sense—besides Thomas, she figured their intimate life was typical of every other married couple. It seemed … adequate. Thomas never forced himself on her and if she declined his amorous advances, he never pursued her. Since he never demanded, she often went along with his desire just to please him. All-in-all, their bedroom activities had been—the same word came to Hallie's mind … adequate.

Hallie had a feeling that nothing with Cooper would ever be just adequate. Even now, watching him, her heart hammered and her breathing quickened.

"Hallie, are you going to stare a hole in my back? Or is there something you want to say?" Cooper called without turning around.

She inhaled sharply. "I don't know what you're talking about."

Cooper chuckled. "Okay, have it your way."

After several minutes, she said, "Well, I do have a question." She hastened to add, "but you don't have to answer if you don't want to."

Typical of Cooper, he answered, "Shoot."

In spite of her nervousness, Hallie smiled. "I know that you were a soldier in the war, but what did you do before that?"

Cooper was quiet for so long she was about to apologize for overstepping her bounds, when he answered, "I worked for large ranches driving longhorns to market. Mostly the drives were along the Shawnee Trail from Texas to Missouri."

Hallie chanced another question? "Were you born in either of those states?"

"Yes—West Texas."

"Do you miss being there?"

"Sometimes."

Thus far their discussion went on without Cooper turning around.

Hallie didn't know what possessed her but she suddenly blurted, "Have you ever been married?"

Cooper paused, continued walking, but still didn't turn around. "Why do you want to know?"

Hallie couldn't believe she'd been so brazen and wanted to crawl under a rock, but there were no rocks in sight. Instead of apologizing, however, sudden indignation came to her rescue.

"I'm just making conversation. Usually, when people are around each other day after day they converse. It's a simple question, but I see that I've offended you, so I withdraw the question. Instead, I'll ask another one. What genus of grass to you suppose it is that we're walking on?"

Cooper came to a sudden halt and slowly turned around. Hallie prepared herself for his wrath at her unreasonable, biting words. Instead, laughter lines creased the sides of his mouth and eyes.

Still feeling indignant, she scowled at him.

"Yes. I've been married." His mouth quirked, "and divorced."

Hallie's mouth formed a circle. "Oh. I'm so sorry. I-I didn't mean to pry. I just wanted to make conversation."

Cooper laughed loudly. "Is there anything else you want to know?"

Embarrassment in the shade of deep pink crept up Hallie's complexion. "No. No. Nothing." *Liar*.

Chapter 18: Platte Incident

After the monotony of rolling hills and grasslands, the train finally arrived at Fort Kearney. Hallie expected a grand military fort, but instead, found several unpainted wooden structures encasing a center square, with a scattering of trees surrounding it. In contrast to many long sod buildings haphazardly fanning out from the wooden ones, the first sorry buildings actually appeared inviting. Between the trees, various artillery equipment sat sentinel. Facing each other on opposite sides of the square were the commander's home and the soldiers' barracks, both two stories high. The other wooden buildings turned out to be officers' quarters, a hospital, and a sutler's store.

Captain Jones called camp a short distance outside the fort and many of the emigrants took the opportunity to visit and replenish supplies. At dusk, the captain called a general meeting to discuss current "Important Particulars."

Excitement fairly sizzled when he boomed from the center of the gathering, "May I have everyone's attention!" The buzz of voices ceased while they waited to hear what he had to say. "Reaching Fort Kearney has brought us to the three hundred mile mark in our journey and not quite a month on the trail. Now, so as to stay on schedule, we'll be picking up the pace after leaving the fort."

He pushed his hat back, changed his mind and removed it, slapped it against his thigh, and scanned the circle. He continued matter-of-factly. "Other than a few broken axles, one river crossing incident, and several disagreements among ya'll, we've had no serious setbacks. But our travels are about to get tougher. We're only a few miles south of the Platte River and we'll be following it, which includes the North Platte, for over three hundred miles. Just so you know, the Platte is not a gracious river. It's muddy and unpredictable. So don't let its shallowness fool you. Its currents and quicksand are treacherous.

"As for using the water, you're gonna have to sift the mud out. I sure hope you took my advice and stocked your barrels with good water at our previous stops."

Again, he dusted his hat on his thigh and Hallie slid her gaze sideways toward Cooper, thankful they had done everything requested by the captain.

After breaking camp the next morning, Hallie fortified herself emotionally for the coming journey. Her body already felt strong from all the walking, but she wondered if she was emotionally ready for what lay ahead. *I can do this. I can face whatever lies ahead.* Hearing Cooper's crack of the whip and cry of, "Giddup," she suddenly felt invincible. *With Cooper's guidance, Tim and I can do this.*

It didn't take long to reach the Platte and Hallie's first glimpse revealed a broad, muddy, slow moving river occasionally interspersed with islands. Although the captain had said it was only four inches deep in some places, the depth was impossible to determine through the murky water. Hallie shuddered at the possibility of quicksand, remembering an incident from her childhood.

She and her sister had traveled with their parents several miles from their home to bring supplies donated by their church to a widow and her teenage son. While Hallie and Lilah played pick-up-sticks with the son in front of the fireplace, the widow had conversed with her parents at the table and described her husband's death in quicksand on their move from Tennessee. Her descriptions had been highly detailed and when the woman cried, "My boy barely escaped the same fate trying to rescue his pa," Hallie had seen tears in his eyes. Then the woman sobbed, "Quicksand is the gate to the pits of hell!"

Hallie shuddered again and turned to Tim, admonishing him to never go near the river without her or Cooper. She finished with, "Promise?"

"I promise, Ma."

After a long day of following the Platte, they reached a much used campsite, which they shared with another train. The pioneers from both groups welcomed the opportunity to mingle and before long about a half dozen men had pulled out fiddles, and several others— including a woman—harmonicas. The musicians started a lively tune and were soon joined by a large-boned woman with frizzy gray hair, carrying her guitar. One of the older couples in Hallie's group, quiet and unassuming, joined the festivities and stood in front of the musicians, surprising everyone with their beautiful voices and rich harmonies. A few jugs of whiskey were privately passed around, which loosened the limbs of several couples, and soon young and old were dancing country jigs.

Hallie smiled at the festivity and glanced around for Cooper. Her gaze landed on Mrs. Pittance with her perpetually sour face and disapproving glare. Sighing, she looked beyond her and saw Cooper leaning against a wagon, the tip of his cigarette glowing as he took a draw on it. Sensing she was watching him, his eyes shifted to hers and he tipped the brim of his hat in a friendly gesture. Hallie nodded slightly, feeling embarrassed that he had caught her seeking him out.

A tug on her arm brought her around. Tim asked, "Ma, will you dance with me?"

Hallie hadn't danced since the last barn raising she and Tim had attended with Thomas, and the memory of that lovely day brought a wave of sadness. Tim loved dancing so, not wanting to disappoint him, she said, "I'd be proud to dance with you."

He grinned, lightly encircling her waist with one hand and holding her hand with his other. They had only danced a few seconds when the song ended, but another one quickly took its place. The lively tune brought laughter from Hallie, and Tim said, "Ma, I'm always going to remember this night."

* * *

Cooper took another drag of his cigarette and watched Hallie dancing with her son. When she tilted her head back and laughed at something Tim said, he admired her long, graceful neck. In the firelight, her skin glowed pink. A few escaped tendrils of hair, the color of sandalwood, lay possessively over one breast, the same breast he had seen the night of her bath; the breast he wanted to smooth his rough palm over to feel its softness. *Slow down, Cooper. Change the direction of your thoughts.*

A nearby sound pulled his gaze away from Hallie. *Oh hell!*

"Hello, Cooper," Clarissa practically purred. She wasn't alone. "I'd like you to meet Sharon."

Sharon, closer to Cooper's age and showing the toll of her profession, ran a finger across her lips and down her neck to the swell of her breasts. "It's a pleasure meeting you, Cooper. We've spoken a few times when you checked our wagon for mechanical problems…but that's not the same as a personal chat, and there's nothing like a hoedown for getting to know someone." She reached a hand and stroked it across Cooper's chest, leaving no doubt as to her meaning.

Cooper took a final drag on his cigarette, almost burning his fingers, before flipping it to the ground and grinding it with his boot heel, studying the movement. Glancing back up, he decided truthfulness was his best line of defense. "Ladies, I hope you don't take this the wrong way because I'm right honored by your attention, and you and your companions are mighty desirable, but I'm not inclined to partake of any distractions while on this train. I need to keep all my faculties about me." He paused before finishing, "Are you gettin' my meaning?"

Clarissa frowned, looking petulant, but Sharon smiled, cast a glance in Hallie's direction, and said, "Oh, yes, I'm seeing your meaning."

Now it was Cooper's turn to frown.

Sharon stepped closer until her breasts grazed his chest, giving him a look he figured was intended to

135

show him all he was missing. In a husky voice, she said, "It's your loss, Cooper. But if you change your mind, me and Clarissa are only a few wagons away."

Cooper returned her stare without flinching. "I'll remember that, ma'am." He stepped backward and tipped his hat politely. "Excuse me, ladies."

* * *

When the music ended, Hallie said breathlessly, "Tim, thank you for the lovely dance!"

"I had fun, Ma." Already his attention was directed across the camp. "Can I go play to my friends?"

"Of course. Check back with me soon, though."

"Okay, Ma."

Hallie waved a hand to cool her burning face, not sure if it was from the exertion of dancing or having been caught by one of the fancy ladies watching Cooper. The fancy woman had shifted her gaze from Cooper toward Hallie and smiled, as if they shared a secret. Embarrassed, Hallie had returned a quick smile, not wanting to appear rude.

* * *

By the third day of following the winding, sludgy, Platte River through treeless rolling hills, Hallie distracted her boredom by mentally preparing her land for planting and laying out the floor plan of her new cabin for the thousandth time. The noon break interrupted her daydream and after lunch cleanup, she settled into the back of her wagon to rest before Captain Jones again called for departure. However, restlessness soon had her up again. She decided to join Tim, who was visiting the Hankersons. Cooper had left earlier for a meeting with the leaders.

As happened during the mid day rest, the wagons were not circled, but ran parade style along the Platte, and the Hankersons were at the opposite end of the train from Hallie. When she reached their wagon, no one was around, so she continued her walk a little farther down the banks of the river. The warm sun and gentle breeze soon had her daydreaming again.

The river meandered around a hillock and before she realized, she was out of sight of camp. Just as she was about to turn around, a woman's scream shattered the peaceful day. The terror in the scream jolted Hallie into action and she bolted forward, searching for the source. The woman screamed again and her words sent chills up Hallie's spine. "Someone help me! My baby's in the quicksand."

Rounding the far side of the hill, she came upon a scene that turned her blood cold. A toddler had wandered about thirty feet into the mire of Platte quicksand, his flailing arms only sending him deeper into the mud. His mother, at the edge of the pit, twisted around frantically looking for help, but didn't see Hallie. The poor woman sobbed and started forward to save her child. Just as Hallie started to yell at her not to enter the mud, Tim appeared at the top of the hill, shouting, "I'll get him!"

Now it was Hallie's turn to scream. "No, Tim! Don't go in the quicksand!"

By now the child was up to his tummy and crying pitifully. Tim glanced over his shoulder, saw his mother, but didn't slow his progress. He waded in toward the child.

Hallie reached the mother and jerked her around. "Run to camp and get help!" The woman appeared not to hear and continued her hysterics. When she attempted to break free of Hallie's grasp and rush into the mud again, Hallie was left with no option but to slap her hard across the cheek. She knew there was little time. "Run to camp and get help!"

The young mother gulped air, focused on Hallie for a second, and then took off running like the wind.

Hallie lifted her head to the heavens. *What now?*

Bringing her gaze back to the children, she yelled to Tim that help was coming. He was now beside the child and lifting him into his arms. But as the boy's body came out of the mud, Tim sunk to his thighs. Frantically glancing along the banks of the river, Hallie searched for anything in the treeless land to assist in saving them. On her second pass, she blinked to be sure she was looking at a miracle—a partially buried tree limb. Running to retrieve it, she tugged, but it was stuck in the reeds and mud.

She yelled at Tim. "I found a tree limb. Hang on. Make your body relax. If you fight the mud, you'll sink faster."

Vaguely, she saw Tim trying to calm the terrified child. On her knees she clawed at the sludge holding the limb fast and used all of her strength to try to tug it from the mire. Her muscles burned, but she wouldn't stop. Finally, with a sucking sound, it broke free and she fell backward. She quickly regained her footing, but determined the branch wasn't long enough to reach the children. She pushed her petticoat down to her knees, but she was shaking so bad, and her skirt so mud laden, she had trouble stepping out of it. She cried, "Help me, Lord. Help me, Lord."

Using all of her strength yet again, she ripped a side seam from top to bottom and jerked the fabric from her body. Next, she tied one end of the petticoat around one end of the limb. Even as she worked, she waded deeper into the Platte, praying she could get within tossing distance of the children before reaching quicksand herself. She swung the limb forward hoping the cloth would reach the children. Her first attempt fell short. Drawing the limb and fabric back, now muddy and heavier, she inhaled, held her breath, glanced at the heavens, prayed again, and tossed again.

This time the end of the petticoat was close enough for Tim to grab onto. She yelled, "I'm going to start walking backward. Hang on tight."

Slowly, she retreated until a taunt line was created between herself and her son. The toddler screamed and started fighting, so she paused and waited while Tim attempted to quiet the boy. The child threw himself backward and Hallie's body shook with fear. Tim and the child both sunk to their waists.

Cooper, I need you!

Suddenly, the child stilled and reached for the fabric himself. Now both children hung on for dear life. Hallie began walking backward again and the children began sliding out of the quicksand. Slowly. Slowly.

Without warning, the fabric snapped off the branch and Hallie fell onto the muddy bank. "No!" she screamed. The quicksand was just below the children's chests. She tried to scramble to her feet, but fell again. Finally, lifting her soggy skirt and regaining her feet, she ran toward them. There was nothing left but for her to go in after them, even though she knew in her heart they would all die.

Suddenly, she was clasped around the waist by strong arms.

Cooper yelled. "No, Hallie, I've got them!"

Relief beyond anything imaginable flooded Hallie's heart and she sobbed, "I knew you'd come!"

Other shouts rang out and within a heartbeat Cooper was wading toward the children with a rope tied around his chest. Grabbing a child in each arm, they clung to him while men from their camp pulled the rope and hauled them all out of the mire.

Immediately, they were surrounded by helpful pioneers and the child's mother grabbed her son to her breast, sobbing. Dazed by the encounter, Hallie finally came to herself and rushed to Tim, clutching him and weeping. He clung to her and softly cried. No words were necessary. Then he pushed back and said, "Ma, I'm sorry for disobeying and leaving camp. I saw a baby deer and I was chasing it." Wiping a hand across his face and slinging mud aside, he sniffed and gave a little smile. "We need to get the mud off before it dries and we can't move."

Hallie nodded, not trusting herself to speak. She looked toward the bank of the river and saw Cooper watching them. In that moment, nothing existed except his blue gaze and her gratefulness. Covered with sludge, he slowly smiled, his teeth gleaming in the midst of the mud. Without stopping to think, Hallie ran to him, throwing her arms around his neck and kissing him passionately. He hesitated for only a second before returning the kiss, snaking his arms around her waist and pulling her close. Finally breaking away, he glanced past her. "Hallie, we've got an audience."

When she realized what she had done, Hallie gasped and placed a hand over her mouth, her eyes wide. "I'm so sorry, Cooper! I-I just wanted to kiss you…I mean thank you." She lifted a muddy hand to her burning cheek, recognizing the import of what she'd just said. Staring at Cooper's solemn expression on a face as smudged as her own, she didn't know how to fix her blunder.

Cooper looked past her again and said, "Clarissa, can you help Hallie clean up?"

"Oh, yes, of course."

Hallie turned around and was immediately pounced on by the fancy women.

* * *

Cooper watched Clarissa and the other ladies surround Hallie and lead her back to camp. Emmett approached Tim, whose questioning expression was fixed on Cooper, and guided him toward Lydia and Sam.

Beyond them, Cooper saw Mrs. Pittance piercing him with a gaze that said, "I knew it."

Obviously, even a life and death situation would not deter her from her purpose. And he was sure her purpose was to discredit Hallie. He almost laughed in her face. *Good luck. Hallie is now a hero among these people. Her quick thinking bought enough time for help to arrive.*

Slinging mud off his arms, as if ridding himself of Mrs. Pittance's judgment, he turned away.

Captain Jones came up behind him, "That was a close call. Another couple of minutes and we'd be havin' a burial instead of a celebration."

"You got that right."

"That Wells woman's got some guts."

"Yeah."

"Ever think about settling down, Cooper?"

"Jeremiah, don't even go there."

Captain Jones chuckled. "Sure was entertainin' seeing two clumps of mud kissin' like that."

"I'm warning you, Jeremiah."

The Captain only let loose with a belly laugh. "I'll see you back at camp, Cooper."

Chapter 19: Fancy Girlfriends

Absentmindedly, Hallie listened to Clarissa issuing orders and watched the fancy ladies hurrying to carry them out. She held Hallie's hand and talked incessantly, seemingly oblivious to the mud being smeared on her own clothing as she pulled Hallie toward camp. "I just have to say, Hallie, you are the bravest woman I have ever met and I'm mighty proud to know ya."

Hallie only half listened because she couldn't stop thinking about kissing Cooper. What had she done? Now the whole camp would be buzzing with gossip and the thought of it affecting Tim almost had her in tears.

Clarissa kept up her one-sided conversation until they reached camp and the other ladies surrounded them, several speaking at the same time. She suddenly held up her hands and they quieted. "Molly, did you pull out the tub? Sadie, did you unpack my special soap? Is Bessie back from Miz Wells' wagon with a change of clothes?"

The women answered in turn.

"Sure did, Clari. Used the water over the campfire to get the temperature just right."

"Yep. Miz Wells is gonna love your soap and I see Bessie returning now with her clothes."

Suddenly, Clarissa was pushing Hallie to a blanketed-off area and two ladies began unfastening and helping her out of her muddy dress.

Sadie said, "You're gonna feel like a new woman after you soak in our tub. That ol' captain wanted us to leave it behind, but we voted and said there was no way we was gonna do that. No way!"

Before Hallie could voice her approval, she was undressed and pushed into a tub overflowing with bubbles. After the hell of the quicksand, surely she was in heaven. With her eyes closed she relaxed in the warm water. When she peeked from beneath her lashes, Clarissa was pouring water onto her mud caked hair.

"I got the nicest soap for yer hair. You're gonna love it. It's called Lovely Lavender and one of my men bought it for me afore I left on this train. He was right sorry to see me leave. I kinda liked him, but he was a might old for me, bein' in his sixties."

Clarissa prattled on and Hallie inhaled the enticing fragrance while the girl scrubbed her hair. She was suddenly brought out of her lethargy, however, when Clarissa said, "You lied to me, Miz Wells."

"Huh? What? What do you mean?"

Clarissa lifted a bucket of fresh water sitting next to the tub and poured it over Hallie's head to remove the soap and mud. Wiping the water out of her eyes, Hallie repeated. "What did I lie to you about?"

Clarissa smiled conspiratorially. "You said you didn't have feelins' for Mr. Jerome. If me and the other ladies had known the truth, we would'a stopped tryin' to get his attention."

"No, Clarissa, you're wrong. I'm recently widowed and Cooper is just helping me and Tim cross to Oregon. After that, he's returning to his farm in Missouri and we'll never see each other again."

Clarissa rocked back on her heels. "If there's one thing I've learned, it's that the heart can't be tamed. Yer brain might be thinkin' one thing but yer heart another. Havin' feelings for Cooper ain't nothin' to be ashamed of. He's a rightly good man and one of the handsomest I've had the pleasure of lookin' on. That's a combination sure to make any woman lose her heart. Besides, any husband in his right mind would want his woman to find a good man after his demise. I bet yer dead husband would want you and Mr. Jerome to hitch up."

Big tears welled in Hallie's eyes. "No, Clarissa. It just wouldn't be right with Thomas being dead so recently. Besides, Cooper wouldn't give me a second glance. I'm too plain and skinny. You…you go after him if you want." The events of the day and Clarissa's ability to hone in on the thoughts troubling Hallie caused her to stifle a sob.

Clarissa clucked. "Nope, Hallie, you got it all wrong. Mr. Jerome's got feelins' for you. Why, when me and Sharon tried to entice him into our bed the night of the hoedown, he just looked in yer direction and excused hisself." She grinned widely. "There ain't no man right in the head that's gonna turn down me and Sharon lessen' he's got another woman on his mind."

As if saying her name had conjured her up, Sharon slipped behind the blankets with a towel. "Here's a towel, Clari. I got some hot water going for tea so Miz Wells can relax when she gets out."

"Thanks, Sharon."

Sharon glanced at Hallie and grinned. "I gave it my damndest and he wasn't budging." Without a word of explanation, she winked and slipped back outside the blankets.

Later that night, the toddler's parents entered Hallie's campsite and introduced themselves as Paul and Charlene Ludlow. Sitting atop his father's shoulders, Little Paul pointed at Tim and said, "Candy?"

They all peered at Tim, who laughed. "Oh, yeah, I almost forgot. Excuse me a minute." He returned shortly with a huge lollypop that his father had given him and handed it to the child.

Hallie was shocked that he was giving away something so precious to him, and that he was doing so without first receiving permission from the child's parents. But before she could chastise him, he explained, "The only way I could get him to stop struggling when we were sinking in the quicksand was to promise him the biggest lollypop he'd ever seen."

The boy whooped when he grasped the lollypop and his parents brushed tears from their eyes. With a heartfelt tremor in his voice, Mr. Ludlow said, "Thank you, Tim. We are forever in your debt." He turned to Hallie, "And in yours and Cooper's too."

Chapter 20: Descending Windlass Hill

Over the next several days, Hallie reflected on her experience and felt a growing sense of the unpredictability of life. One minute life was rolling along fine, and the next, a life or death situation reared its head. Tim also seemed reflective for a boy so young. He often discussed the rescue with his mother and Cooper, and on one occasion broke down crying. "I didn't want to die, Ma, but I could feel the mud sucking me under. I was so scared."

Hallie tried to comfort him. "I know, son. I was scared, too. But I think it's during times of fear that we find our greatest strength. Something else I've learned is that we can never take our lives for granted." Hugging him tightly, she whispered, "We've got this one life; let's enjoy it to the fullest. That's what your pa did. He loved life and even though his was cut short, he appreciated every day."

Cooper, meanwhile, never mentioned Hallie's impulsive kiss and kept mostly to himself. At times, Hallie found herself wanting to bring up the subject and apologize for embarrassing him in front of everyone, but something held her back. Apologizing almost made the kiss seem wrong, and deep in her heart, she couldn't make herself believe that.

They reached Fort McPherson almost two weeks later and after that traveled along a stretch called O'Fallon's Bluff. Again, they had to trek single file because of rocks butted so close to the Platte River. At a place known as the Lower California Crossing they forded the Platte with only minor damage to a few wagons.

That night Captain Jones explained at an "Important Particulars" meeting that the next twenty-five miles would be high plains. He warned, "There's very little wood, so collect buffalo chips for kindling. Also, your wagon wheels are going to shrink. They expanded during our travel along the banks of the Platte, but the dry plains wreak havoc on the wood. Have lots of shims ready to keep the inner and outer wheels tight."

Before ending the meeting, Captain Jones scratched his beard and said, "Folks, just so you know, we're over four hundred miles from Westport."

A happy shout arose among the pioneers and they hugged each other.

He continued, "It's good to be happy, but don't become lazy. We're not even halfway to Oregon and disasters can strike in the blink of an eye, like what almost happened with Tim and Little Paul."

It took two full days to cross twenty-five miles of plains and although rumors ran amok that their next destination was a treacherous place called Windlass Hill, Captain Jones neither verified nor denied the rumors when asked flat out. All he said was, "One day at a time, folks."

When they reached Windlass Hill, those at the head of the train sent runners back to the others describing a place of dread. It was no wonder Captain Jones hadn't elaborated on what was to come.

Calling the pioneers together, he chuckled, "So, ladies and gents, as you can see, it's decision time. I'm going to lay out our options and let you vote on what to do because either decision is fine with me.

"First, we can descend the three hundred feet of Windlass Hill, which means our oxen or mules will pull the wagons as far as possible, then we'll release them to find their way to the bottom while we tie ropes to the wagons, set the brakes, and with men holding the ropes in back and other men in front steering the tongue, guide the wagons to the bottom. And let me assure you, it's been done many times over the years without mishap. Our other option is to continue on about seventeen miles out of our way and then backtrack. Of course, if we take the longer route, we lengthen our travel time and chance meeting the winter snows if we encounter other hindrances. Lowering the wagons will take less time than traveling the long way," he paused and glanced from face-to-face, "unless we have a serious accident."

The pioneers glanced uncertainly around at each other. Hallie wondered how Cooper would vote.

Captain Jones said, "Okay, I need a showing of hands and women can vote since their lives and the lives of their children are on the line. Only those over seventeen can vote unless you're already married. Ya'll spread out so's I can count."

Nervously, the emigrants fanned out and Captain Jones asked, "How many think we should take the long way?"

Hallie looked around and watched hands lift. She felt Mrs. Pittance's eyes on her and glanced over to see her hand raised halfway, but once Cooper lifted his hand, the woman lowered hers, causing some of the folks in her group to do the same. Pastor Pittance stood to the side observing.

Following Cooper's lead, Hallie raised her hand.

Captain Jones counted and then said, "Okay, all those in favor of following the trail down Windlass Hill, raise your hands."

Mrs. Pittance lifted her hand high, which encouraged others in her group to raise theirs also. Hallie looked at Pastor Pittance. Again, he only observed.

Captain Jones counted and said, "It's a close call. Only three votes difference." He glanced around the group and his eyes settled in the Pittances' direction. "Looks like, folks, ya'll better secure your wagons."

Under Captain Jones's direction, the wagons were prepared for the steep descent down Windlass Hill. Below the hill, the place called Ash Hollow with beautiful trees and tall grasses could be seen. It was as if hell had to be overcome before they could partake of paradise.

As the crowd of emigrants huddled at the top of the hill—watching and praying—the lead wagon, belonging to Frank Jensen, descended. The incline became too steep for the oxen about halfway down, and the men in front position, which included Cooper, unhitched them. Two of the men followed the oxen to the bottom while Cooper and three others, holding the tongue, guided the wagon, and men in back held ropes tied to the frame. When the schooner touched level land, a unified shout arose from those watching atop the hill.

The next wagon moved to the descending point and again, breaths were held and prayers offered. After the successful descent of ten wagons, many of the emigrants lost interest and went to find other diversions until it was their turn.

With twenty wagons still ahead of Hallie's, she walked back to double-check everything. She gave permission for Tim to accompany a family with six boys to their wagon and play, wanting him to have a diversion other than watching the precarious descent of wagons and animals.

After making sure everything was secure, she walked back to the crest of the hill and sat on a boulder just as another wagon began its descent. She thought about her fellow travelers. Since the incident with the toddler, several emigrants had approached her, Tim, and Cooper in a friendly manner, offering their help with anything they might need.

When Harley and Stubby's pitiful wagon and animals moved to front position, Hallie's attention was quickly returned to the present. Unbidden resentment filled her heart.

The men secured the wagon in the same fashion that had successfully lowered the ones before, and for all of Stubby's and Harley's outward appearance of sloth, they attacked their duty to lower their wagon with gusto.

About twenty feet into the descent, there was a loud cracking sound and one of the men guiding the mules yelled, "Runaway wagon!"

Hallie's jumped to her feet and stared in horror as the wagon slid sideways, tilted precariously, and then careened down the hillside, pulling its four mules with it. Several of the women watching from the top of the bluff screamed when Harley, unable to jump clear, got tangled in the reins and tumbled with the mules and wagon. As if in a nightmare, the emigrants watched Harley being dragged down the precipice. Stubby yelled and attempted to descend the grade, but the men held him back.

When the wagon and the animals and Harley finally hit the bottom, a deathly quiet rang out, its silence louder than any noise would have been. Everyone stood frozen in disbelief, until Stubby's heartrending scream, "Harley!" goaded people into action.

The men at the bottom of Windlass Hill rushed to the scene and others started descending. The sound of mules screaming floated to the top of the hill.

By now, word of the disaster had spread and emigrants ran to the edge of the bluff. Gunfire suddenly blasted, once, twice, thrice, and then once more; the mules ceased their screams.

There was a shout from one of the men at the bottom. "Harley's dead! Neck's broke!"

Another heart wrenching cry erupted from Stubby and some of the men had to pull him back atop the bluff where fell to his knees and wailed, "He's my only kin and friend."

Seeing the pioneers' mouths agape at the dreadful happening, Hallie's gaze fell on Mrs. Pittance. She looked impassive. She even shook her head as if to say, "You had this coming." When she turned and walked away, some of the others in her group did the same. Pastor Pittance only observed, but did not follow them.

Any resentment Hallie had toward Stubby evaporated, at least for the time being. Looking back at his crouched and weeping form, Hallie took a step toward him, but he was suddenly surrounded by the fancy women. Mrs. Martinique was the first to kneel beside him and lay a comforting hand on his shoulder. Within minutes, the ladies had coaxed him away from the scene, his sobs tearing at Hallie's heart.

* * *

The rest of the day was incident free except for some broken wheel spokes, a few sprained ankles and shoulders, and some gashes to arms and legs. Finally, at dusk, the last wagon safely reached the bottom and all of the emigrants had maneuvered the steep decline to the lush grasses and trees and crystal clear water below.

Cooper collapsed onto a rock in exhaustion, but was soon called upon to help move Harley's body away from camp and dig his grave. As night deepened, the pioneers, carrying lanterns, gathered respectfully at the last resting place of a man lowly regarded by them.

Captain Jones asked Pastor Pittance if he wanted to say something, and the pastor simply said, "We know not the heart of this man; only God does. He has been sent to his final reward. Amen."

In the lamplight a frown could be seen on the captain's face. He glanced around and asked, "Does anyone else have anything to say?"

After a silence, Stubby's voice cracked when he said, "Harley was me older cousin and we growed up tagather. He weren't always upright, but he always looked out fer me. If'n you were raised by a pa that always beat the hell outta ya and taught ya to steal and cheat, ya would'na been so upstandin' yerself." Stubby choked on his next words, "Harley was me friend."

Clarissa placed her hand on Stubby's shoulder and with the innocence of youth, said, "You'll make new friends, Stubby."

Stubby rubbed his nose with the back of his fist and nodded.

Captain Jones said in his loud voice, now tempered with compassion, "I'm callin' a meeting. Everyone gather in the center of camp pronto."

Cooper gave one last glance at Harley as men shoveled dirt on him, pondering what Stubby had said.

Back at camp, a subdued atmosphere hovered while everyone waited to hear what Captain Jones had to say. He stepped to the center and boomed. "We got a situation now of a man without a wagon, animals, or supplies. We salvaged what we could from his goods, but it weren't much. So…pioneers, who'll be the first to help Stubby?"

Uneasy fidgeting and silence accompanied the captain's request. Mrs. Martinique was the first to speak. "Stubby can join with my gals."

A gasp arose among the crowd and then Stubby said, "I thank you ma'am, but I'll not live on the skirts of women. I'm not–"

Hallie interrupted. "I have an extra ox that Stubby can have and food to share."

Cooper blinked in disbelief.

Stubby frowned and started to say something, but Captain Jones looked pointedly at him and ordered,

"Don't say anything!" Then he turned his gaze on Hallie. "Now that's right neighborly of you, Miz Wells." He sent a hard stare around the gathering. "Anyone else?"

Mr. Liverman yelled from the back of the group, "I got a small cart that could easily be pulled by one ox. Stubby can have it."

After that, pioneers from every direction began calling out what they had to offer.

Captain Jones finally lifted his hand and said, "Okay, looks like we got Stubby outfitted quite well. Tomorrow morning, bring your offerings to the back of Mrs. Martinique's wagons." He glanced at Cooper and said, "Cooper, you can help Stubby get his ox harnessed and his supplies readied for the journey. We'll rest here for another day."

Cooper simply nodded and said, "Yes, sir."

Chapter 21: Eyeful at Ash Hollow

Hallie decided that Captain Jones had been wise in not pushing the emigrants to leave Ash Hollow immediately. The descent down Windlass Hill and Harley's subsequent death had placed melancholia over the group, not to mention the fact that exhaustion played a major factor in their depressed state.

Soon, however, the beauty of their surroundings performed magic in renewing their spirits. Shade trees, which made for abundant firewood, covered the landscape, plentiful grass fattened their animals, and pristine waters flowed.

By noon of their first day of rest, Cooper had Stubby's cart loaded and ox ready to be tethered. From across the camp, Hallie watched Stubby call to Cooper as he turned to leave. Cooper paused and listened to something Stubby said and then the two men shook hands. When Stubby started toward Hallie's campsite, she wanted to run away. She may have given him an ox and supplies because it was the charitable thing to do, but she surely didn't want to talk to him.

She said, "Tim, run over to the Hankersons and see if they need help gathering firewood."

Always ready to visit Sam, Tim said, "Sure, Ma," and took off running.

Hallie straightened her dress and folded her hands in her lap. Cooper was walking behind Stubby.

Near the edge of the imaginary border to her campsite, Stubby paused, looked at his boots, and finally glanced up sheepishly. He looked surprisingly different after bathing and shaving and Hallie suspected the fancy women had had something to do with his sudden change in appearance.

He cleared his throat once, and then again. "Ah, Miz Wells, I…ah…want to thank you fer yer kindness. After what I done, most folks would'a turned their backs on me. But you're a right kind woman and…and I'm well and truly sorry for my sorry-ass behavior. I get right obnoxious when I drink, so I'm tryin' ta change that wickedness by not indulgin' in liquor no more." During his speech he looked everywhere except in Hallie's eyes, but now he shifted his gaze to hers and said earnestly, "I'm just sorry it took losin' Harley to open me eyes."

When Stubby visibly swallowed and his Adam's apple bobbed, Hallie realized just how difficult this apology was for him.

With the hint of a smile, she said, "Stubby, I only wish the best for you and I'm truly sorry about Harley. I know how it is to lose someone you love dearly." She fingered a tear.

Stubby swiped his own eyes and said quickly, "Thanks, ma'am." He turned and started walking away so quickly, he almost ran into Cooper.

* * *

Resting under a tree, Cooper closed his eyes and fought his desire for Hallie. The smile she'd given Stubby earlier was one of the sweetest he'd ever seen. Why he'd ever thought her plain, he had no idea. Every day she became more beautiful and even though Mrs.

Martinique's gals had made it clear they were available to him anytime, he had no desire for any of them.

Pressing his fingers to his forehead, he squeezed his eyes tight. *Cooper, how could you let this happen?*

After a time, he gathered firewood and returned to camp. He had seen Hallie headed in the direction of the Hankersons earlier and figured she was still gone. Walking to the back of the wagon, he reached to move the flap so he could drop an armful of firewood in the box. He looked up and lost all the air in his lungs. Standing in profile and bent over at the waist, Hallie rubbed a damp cloth up her calf. Wearing only a thin shift that had fallen away at the bodice, and with her hair unbound and cascading to the wooden planks, she was tantalizing beyond description.

As if in slow motion, she turned her head and met his gaze. He couldn't make his legs move, but his eyes sure did, traveling up and down the graceful lines of her slim form, following every curve, and finally settling on her breasts. Then, without apology, he met her gaze again before closing the flap. He dumped the wood on the ground and walked out of camp and back to the same tree he had just come from. Pulling tobacco and paper from his pocket, he rolled a smoke.

* * *

Hallie couldn't breathe and when she could, it was so rapid she got lightheaded. Quickly donning her dress, she hastened to cover herself. Never had a man looked at her the way Cooper had—not even her husband. Thomas had watched her dress, of course, and complimented her figure, but Cooper's look had been, for want of better words—hotter than the fires of hell.

Hallie knew beyond a shadow of a doubt that if he had touched her, she would have vanished in a puff of smoke. And, heaven help her, she'd wanted him to touch her.

Raising a trembling hand to the pulse in her throat, she felt its rapid staccato. *I'm so sorry, Thomas. I'm so sorry he makes me want things…* She couldn't even finish her thought.

* * *

An hour later, Cooper returned to camp just as Hallie was pouring hot coffee in a tin. He knew she'd heard his return because she paused in the pouring. Quietly, he said, "I'd sure like a cup."

Just as quietly, she replied, "Here, you can have this one," and handed him the tin, wrapped in a cloth because it was so hot. Accepting it, his fingers grazed hers and she quickly removed her hand.

When their eyes connected, a silent pact was made—there would be no mention of what had happened. Reaching to stir the beans, she said, "Supper will be ready in a few minutes."

"Sure smells good." He walked to the back of the wagon, leaned against it, sipped his coffee, and gazed out amongst the circle of wagons. Finally, he asked, "Where's Tim?"

"He's eating supper with the Hankersons. Seems one of the Liverman boys loaned him a dime novel about Davy Crockett and with Emmett's help, he's been reading it to Sam." She stirred the beans again and then began ladling scoops into a bowl, topping it with hardtack. Walking to the wagon, she set it on the tailgate and then returned to dish her own.

Cooper reached for the bowl and finished the beans in a couple of minutes. "If you'll excuse me, I'll take care of the animals."

Chapter 22: Release at Register Cliff

"Ma! Look at those rocks!" Tim pointed.

Hallie responded, "I'm seeing them but not believing them. I've never seen anything like it. When Captain Jones said we would be passing Courthouse Rock and Jailhouse Rock, I never imagined anything so grand."

Tim pointed again, "And look at those over there!"

Hallie followed the direction he pointed. "Tim, why don't we try to find our own shapes in the formations? We can give them names, too."

"That's a great idea, Ma. I already see an Indian face."

For the next hour, Hallie and Tim pointed out other shapes and named them.

By late afternoon, they came within sight of another grand formation that simply dropped their jaws. The wagons had paused because a wheel had popped off the lead schooner and several pioneers were repairing it. Cooper leaned against the side of their wagon and said, "That's Chimney Rock—quite impressive."

"It certainly is." Hallie marveled at the conical mound rising above the plain with a column shooting high above it, as if stretching to touch a cloud. She glanced from the rock to Cooper and his blue eyes started her heart hammering erratically. Quickly returning her gaze to the formation, she asked, "How long until we reach it?"

"Probably two or three days."

Two days later, Hallie listened to Captain Jones at the impromptu meeting he'd called, making everyone curious about the nature of it. The captain boomed, "Our next major landmark is Scott's Bluff. It used to be pioneers had to travel around it by way of Robidoux Pass, but around 1850 a way through opened up called Mitchell Pass. You'll see the bluff long before we reach it. Now the reason I'm sayin' this is because it's gonna look formidable."

When the pioneers glanced nervously at each other, the captain smiled encouragingly. "But, seein's as to how far we've come, and how many pioneers have traveled this way afore us, it's just a little inconvenience." He grinned and laughed. "Do I make myself clear?"

The Captain's jovial attitude was infectious and a sigh of relief could be heard along with accompanying laughter and, "Yes, sir!"

* * *

By noon of the following day, Cooper glanced beyond Scott's Bluff, still in the distance, to the beginnings of the Rocky Mountains. The foothills would soon give way to towering mountains and their journey would become more arduous. Considering the journey ahead, he decided to change the axle after leaving Scott's Bluff, but before reaching South Pass that would lead them through the Rockies.

Behind him, he heard Hallie and Tim planning the home they would build in Oregon, and although it put a smile on his face, sadness overcame him. As much as he had tried to remain aloof, Hallie and Tim had burrowed their way into his heart. A vision of Hallie bending forward, with her body exposed, taunted him. If he had his druthers, he would send Tim to spend the night with the Hankersons, climb into the wagon with Hallie, and intoxicate them both all night with caresses and kisses. He sighed. *Not gonna happen. You're no good when it comes to family.*

That night the pioneers camped at the base of Scott's Bluff and early the next morning began their ascent through Mitchell Pass, basically a gash in the bluff that would lead them through the midst of towering cliffs. The animals, accustomed to the plains they had been traveling for weeks, balked at first, but soon acquiesced to their masters. At the crest, Captain Jones halted the lead schooner and rode the length of the train, checking wagons and animals. After speaking briefly with Cooper, he moved on and Cooper gazed back across the plains of the Nebraska Territory.

In the distance, a black, shifting mass captured his attention. Immediately he knew what he was seeing. He walked back to Hallie and Tim and pointed. "You're looking at thousands of buffalo."

Hallie placed one hand over her heart and her other on Cooper's arm. "This is truly the adventure of a lifetime. No matter what happens, I shall never regret my decision to continue on to Oregon. I cannot imagine a life of not beholding the wonders of America."

Cooper covered her hand still on his arm, and together they watched unfathomable numbers of buffalo migrate across the plains.

Captain Jones rode back to the lead wagon and soon a shout of, "Westward Ho!" was heard. Cooper released Hallie's hand and they continued onward.

Reaching the far side of the bluff didn't take the entire day, so they kept going until they again met the south bank of the North Platte River.

Circling the wagons for the night, the atmosphere crackled with satisfaction of another accomplishment in the pioneers' long journey. They had traversed the plains and although still a long ways away, now looked forward with excitement and trepidation to the approach of the Rocky Mountains.

* * *

"Look, Ma, there's Fort Laramie." Tim spotted the fort in the distance, named after trapper Jacques LaRamee, whom Cooper said may have been the first white man to visit the area.

"I see it." Hallie ruffled Tim's hair. "We've reached another milestone, son."

Tired and weary, the pioneers circled their wagons outside the fort, but since the sun had yet to set, curiosity led many of them to check it out. Hallie and Tim readily agreed to explore the inside with Cooper. All-in-all, the stronghold was well laid out with an impressive trading post.

While Hallie was perusing the supplies of pots and pans on a far wall, and Tim was deciding on a piece of candy, she saw a military man approach Cooper, who was lifting and weighing several chains in his hands. Surreptitiously, she listened and watched their conversation.

The middle-aged officer said, "Cooper Jerome? Is that you?"

Cooper turned at the man's voice and recognition brought a smile to his face. "Lieutenant English, good to see you."

Lieutenant English replied, "Since you're now a civilian, just call me Smiley."

Hallie turned her head to hide her amusement. Smiley's nickname was obvious. He had a grin that stretched from ear-to-ear with huge, brilliant, buck teeth.

"When did you get assigned to Fort John?" Cooper asked, calling it by its military designation.

"About a year ago when the Indian risings started up again. They're none to happy about all the folks headed west and killing off the buffalo." He lowered his voice, but Hallie could still hear him. "I can understand their frustration. We got some real idiots passing through, especially gold miners. It's like they forget all common sense when gold fever hits 'em."

Cooper nodded. "Yeah, we've got a few of them on our train."

"So you're with Captain Jones's group?"

"That's right. I'm assisting a family on their move to Oregon. Have you spoken to Captain Jones yet?"

"Not yet. The three of us should get together and reminisce old times."

Hallie thought, *Cooper already knew Captain Jones?*

Lieutenant English asked, "When's your train leaving?"

"Probably day after tomorrow."

The lieutenant lowered his voice again and Hallie only heard snatches of his words. "Well … warn you … captured chief's son … stockade … can't be more'n six or seven … Commander … hoping … peace talks … dicey situation. More-n-likely … military escort when you leave."

Lieutenant English glanced in Hallie's direction, who pretended interest in a cast iron skillet. Cooper called, "Hallie, I'd like you to meet a friend of mine."

Hallie looked up, feigning surprise, and saw Cooper's mouth quirk with amusement. *He knows I've been listening.* Rosy color flushed her cheeks as she approached them.

Cooper said, "Lieutenant English, I'd like you to meet Mrs. Hallie Wells. I'm escorting her and her son, Tim, to the Willamette Valley." He motioned toward Tim who was paying for his candy.

The lieutenant removed his cap. "I'm pleased to meet you, ma'am. I visited the Willamette Valley a few years back, before the War of Rebellion, and I can tell you its heaven on earth."

His words sent excitement up Hallie's spine. "It's wonderful to meet someone who's already been there. My husband researched many areas before finally deciding on that particular valley."

Lieutenant English replied, "If you'd like, I can meet with your husband and share what I know."

Hallie glanced quickly at Cooper and back at the lieutenant. "My husband died over two months ago. I hired Cooper to escort my son and me because the dream of Oregon was also my dream."

The lieutenant said, "I'm sorry about your loss, ma'am."

At that moment, the door opened and a young man dressed in uniform said," Lieutenant English, we got issue; the young prisoner is gone."

A shocked expression replaced the lieutenant's jovial smile. "Excuse me, ma'am, Cooper," he said curtly. Without waiting for a response, he stalked out the door.

When Hallie left the trading post with Cooper and Tim, the fort hummed with soldiers entering every building, apparently searching for the escapee.

Before thinking, Hallie said, "I sure hope the child is okay." Clamping her mouth shut, she realized that Cooper now knew for certain she had been eavesdropping.

Cooper responded, with humor in his voice. "He's probably on his way back to his family."

Tim, who had missed the exchange between Cooper and the lieutenant asked, "What prisoner? What boy?"

Cooper ruffled his hair. "This is confidential information. Can I trust you to keep it secret?"

"Yes, sir," Tim said solemnly.

While Cooper explained what Lieutenant English had told him, Hallie berated herself for appearing nosey in Cooper's eyes.

Just as Cooper had said, their train departed the second day after their arrival, and just as Lieutenant English had related to Cooper, a military escort was assigned to them.

There was much speculation among the emigrants about the escaped prisoner and the need for escort. Hallie heard Clarissa telling Stubby, "I heard the prisoner was an Indian over seven feet tall with dozens of scalps hanging from his waist and he was meaner than a starving rattlesnake."

Stubby's eyes rounded and several of the fancy gals stepped closer to him. "Stubby'll keep us safe," Sharon said, winking at Hallie. Stubby seemed to visibly grow taller.

The wagons departed an hour after daylight and a somber mood blanketed the pioneers. The situation appeared serious, what with soldiers flanking their wagons.

At mid morning, Hallie caught Cooper's eye and recognized his expression. He wanted her to rest her feet. Handing the whip to Tim, whom he had been teaching to drive the oxen, he followed Hallie to the back of the wagon and lifted her inside. He told her she needed to rest for at least an hour and then he returned to Tim and the oxen.

Hallie sighed and decided to read the dime novel about Kit Carson that she'd timidly asked to borrow from Cooper. Something about the wagon didn't seem right. Then she realized her trunk was no longer flush against the side panel and a blanket had fallen behind it. Reaching for the blanket, she tugged, but it was stuck. Tugging harder, she finally jerked it loose and stifled a scream. Up jumped a tiny boy wearing a shirt and pants that looked very similar to those Tim had tossed in the dirty clothes duffel bag that morning. The child kept one hand on his pants to hold them up and darted his eyes to the back of the wagon as if about to flee. They assessed each other for several seconds. Finally, Hallie lifted a finger to her lips, indicating they should both remain silent and the boy nodded his understanding.

He flinched slightly when she took a step toward him. She sat on her trunk and leaned to whisper in his ear, "Do you speak English?"

He whispered back, "Little."

"Did you escape the soldiers?"

After a moment's hesitation, the child nodded and Hallie smiled at the expression of pride on his face. The boy grinned back and her heart melted. He couldn't be more than six.

He whispered, "I go home."

Hallie asked, "Do you know how to find your way home?"

The boy nodded and pointed north. "I follow signs. Make animal calls. Father teach."

Hallie pointed to herself. "My name is Hallie."

The child pointed to himself and said an Indian word, and then, "Walking Tall."

"Your name is Walking Tall?"

He nodded and said with all seriousness, "I go when night."

Hallie knew she didn't have it within her to return this little boy to the soldiers who would again place him in the stockade and use him as a pawn in their war. "Yes. But first you must eat."

Moving to the breadbox, she pulled out biscuits from the morning's meal. To that she added some jerky and dried fruit.

The child readily accepted her offering and gobbled the food, apparently starving.

Since the milk canister was fastened to the outside of the wagon, she couldn't give him any of Belle's milk from that morning. Instead, she scooped some water in a tin.

While Walking Tall ate, she searched for one of Tim's belts. Finding one, she approached the boy and whispered, "You're very smart to dress in white man's clothing, but you need something to hold up your pants."

Walking Tall watched as Hallie pushed the belt through the loops of his waistband while he continued to eat hungrily. Next, she turned up the legs of his pants and then the sleeves of his shirt. She whispered, "You're going to need a hat to hide your braids." She reached for Tim's favorite hat that he wore only on special occasions and planted it on the child's head. Leaning back, she observed, "Anyone seeing you after dark will think you're a white child."

The child huffed, "I Indian brave."

Hallie smiled. "Of course you are. But to escape, you must wear a disguise."

The child gave her a look that said he did not understand her word. He reiterated what he had said earlier; "I go when night."

Hallie swallowed the lump in her throat. "Yes, Walking Tall. And I will help you."

Hallie desperately wanted to wet a cloth and wash the boy's dirt-streaked face, but decided it aided his disguise.

When she heard shouts outside the wagon, she motioned for him to hide behind the trunk again and covered him with the blanket. She sat on the trunk just as Tim lifted the back flap. "Ma, some more soldiers just showed up and their talkin' to Captain Jones and the Lieutenant."

Hallie said, "Tim, help me down."

Cooper rounded the wagon and started unleashing Sweet Pea. "I'm going to ride to the front and find out what's happening."

Hallie nodded. When Tim started to climb inside the wagon she asked, "What do you need, son?"

"I was just gonna grab a leftover biscuit."

"That can wait. Run back to the Hankersons and tell them Cooper is checking out the reason for our stopping. When you get back, I'll have a biscuit for you."

Tim gave her a questioning look, but said, "Sure, Ma," and took off running.

Quickly, Hallie opened the milk can, ladled some milk into one of the cups hanging beside the water barrel, and climbed back inside the wagon. Lifting the blanket she whispered, "Drink this and then hide again."

The child downed the milk, creating a milk mustache to go with his dirt streaks, and then ducked behind the trunk once more.

Grabbing a couple of biscuits, Hallie sat on the back of the wagon, dangling her feet over the edge and waiting for Tim and Cooper to return. After a few minutes she heard the trot of a horse and then Cooper rounded the wagon. "The commander of the fort sent word that most of our escort is to return immediately.

Seems there's an increase in braves to the east and he's worried about a war. They need to secure the fort and protect a new train just coming through. He thinks we're far enough west to be out of danger. But just to be sure, Captain Jones wants us to continue without stopping at noon."

Tim returned and hearing Cooper, glanced at his Ma. "Do you want me to go tell the Hankersons?"

Cooper said, "Tim, you can ride with me and we'll alert everyone." He reached down to grasp Tim under the arm and haul him up behind him.

Tim grinned from the back of Cooper's horse and waved to his mother.

Hallie sighed, relieved that they would be gone for awhile.

Because of the threat of Indian trouble, Captain Jones pushed the pioneers onward until dusk and they reached a campsite named Register Cliff. The captain called a meeting with his leaders and the heads of each family, and for that Hallie was glad. The more Cooper was away, the less likely he would discover Walking Tall.

She searched their campsite. The sandstone cliff and rock outcroppings presented the perfect cover for the boy to escape. Once he reached the rocks, he could disappear into the night.

As soon as darkness blanketed the camp, Hallie again sent Tim to the Hankersons; this time with the excuse of asking Emmett if he had finished the other dime novel Cooper had lent him.

Tim gave her a curious look, but obeyed. Quickly, Hallie entered her wagon and whispered, "Walking Tall, it's time for your escape." The child tossed the blanket aside and jumped to his feet. Studying the boy's happy expression, Hallie felt her heart expand. Any doubts about what she was doing evaporated. Blinking back tears, she encircled the tiny boy in a hug and said, "Soon you'll be back with your Ma and Pa where you belong."

The child hesitated, sniffed, and then reached his skinny arms around her waist in a return hug. In that instant, Tim flipped the canvas back and sucked a breath.

Hallie pushed the child behind her and ordered, "Tim, climb inside the wagon and don't make a sound." In the light from their campfire, she watched her son gulp. "Hurry, son! We don't have much time!"

Tim jumped into the wagon and Hallie whispered, "Tim, this is Walking Tall; he's the boy the soldiers were holding in their jail. We need to help him escape so he can return home. It wasn't right for the soldiers to capture him."

Slowly, Tim nodded.

She continued, "I'm going to walk with him to the boulders and I'm hoping anyone who sees us will just think I'm a mother strolling with her child." Hallie reached for Tim's hat and set it on the boy's head, stuffing his braids under it.

Tim's eyes rounded and he said, "Can I trade hats with him?"

"No, honey. After Walking Tall leaves, people might start asking why you're wearing your good hat all the time and we'd have to lie, something we're not good at."

"Okay, Ma. But I got a better idea. After you get him to the rocks, I'll sneak over and walk back with you. Then folks won't wonder why you're coming back alone."

A sudden pride entered Hallie's heart at her son's cleverness. "Yes. That's a great idea. Because it's dark, maybe the difference in your sizes will be less noticeable than me returning by myself." Inhaling deeply to fortify her courage, Hallie continued. "We've got to hurry before Cooper returns."

Tim said, "I'll let you know when it's clear." He jumped from the wagon.

Hallie turned to the boy. "Walking Tall, I want you to know I will never forget you and I wish for peace between our people."

The child, with wisdom shining in eyes beyond his years, nodded his understanding.

Tim slipped his head back inside the flap. "There's no one around right now."

Hallie said, "Okay, son. Keep watching."

While Tim hid behind their wagon, Hallie slipped from it and whispered to Walking Tall, "As soon as I tell you, jump down and hold my hand, and we'll walk toward the rocks. Do you understand?"

The child whispered, "Yes, Hal...Hal-lee."

Hallie walked to her fire, pretending to warm herself, and waited until she felt it was safe to retrieve Walking Tall. Slowly, she walked to the back of her wagon, lifted the canvas and whispered, "Now."

The child jumped to the ground, slipped his hand into her outstretched one, and walked with her toward the boulders. She said, "We can't go too fast." Guiding him to the darkest stretch and with her heart in her throat, she squeezed Walking Tall's hand to encourage him and he returned her squeeze. In just a couple of minutes, though it seemed an eternity, they reached the cover of the rocks. Darting behind them, Hallie said through tears, "You're free, Walking Tall. Run like a deer back to your family."

Hallie heard the child sniff as he released her hand. He started to move away, then quickly turned and embraced her waist. He said, "I love Hal-lee," before disappearing into the night.

Hallie swallowed several times, trying to remove the lump in her throat. A few minutes later she heard Tim calling softly, "Ma?"

"Over here, Tim."

Her son followed the direction of her voice and when he reached her, she said, "Tim, I'm so proud of you. We did what was right." Reaching for her boy, she pulled him into an embrace.

"I know, Ma." He hugged her back.

Chapter 23: Blessing

Because of the threat of Indian attack, Captain Jones pressed the emigrants ever forward, foregoing a stop at Ayres Bridge, a natural formation caused by the erosion of LaPrele Creek. Some of the emigrants already knew about the popular campsite and requested that they make camp there, but the captain's decision to continue onward was respected with few complaints. Every night, he called a meeting to reassure the pioneers that Fort Casper would be reached in a few days.

A day away from their destination, everyone sighed with relief. It looked like they had bypassed Indian hostilities and would reach another safe haven without an encounter.

Alas, it was not to be.

While Hallie daydreamed about planting her first crop, she heard a shout from Emmett as he galloped the length of the train.

"Halt your wagons. Indians ahead!"

Immediately, Cooper called, "Whoa!" and stopped the oxen. He turned and ordered, "Tim, help your mother into the wagon and both of you stay there until I tell you it's safe to come out!"

Tim grabbed his mother's hand and pulled her toward the back of their schooner while Cooper unhitched Sweet Pea and mounted. From inside the wagon, Hallie and Tim peeked around the flap. Because they were close to the front of the train, they had a view of a band of Indians slowly approaching on horseback.

Hallie gasped when she recognized Walking Tall sitting in front of a powerful brave. "Tim, there's Walking Tall. He made it home." She blinked back tears of relief. "Son, I've got to go to the front. Perhaps we can avoid a conflict if Walking Tall sees me."

"Ma, I'm going with you."

"No, son, I want you to stay safe."

"Ma, I'll not let you go alone. I'm the man of the house now and if we're going to die, I want to die with you. I'm not a coward."

Hallie recognized the stubborn set of her son's jaw and pride filled her heart at his courage. She whispered, "We're not going to die, Tim. Walking Tall surely wouldn't be with that brave if they intended to harm us. Besides, we have land waiting for us in Oregon." Then she smiled and grabbed his hand, knowing he would never stay behind. "Come on, we'll face this together." Walking past the wagons in front of theirs, the pioneers gasped.

Cooper, Captain Jones, and the other men sitting atop their horses waiting for the approach of the Indians, heard the commotion and jerked around. An incredulous expression crossed Cooper's face before he rasped, "What the hell are you doing here? Get back to the wagon, pronto!" He started to dismount.

Hallie lifted a hand. "No, Cooper. We know what we're doing." Searching his eyes with her own, she said, "You must trust us."

Cooper sank back into his saddle, his expression registering the fact that he didn't know whether to drag them back to their wagon or trust them.

Hallie looked beyond them to the Indians now within yards of the wagon train's leaders. She made eye contact with Walking Tall and then lifted her gaze to the brave encircling him within his muscular arms. Walking Tall looked upward at the brave, said something, and then pointed at Hallie and Tim. The brave almost smiled. In that instant Hallie knew the emigrants would come to no harm.

Captain Jones, Cooper, and the other men turned their heads back and forth between the Indians and Hallie and Tim. Suddenly, the brave said loudly in broken English, "You go safe with blessing of Great Spirit!" After speaking, he ruffled Walking Tall's hair, nodded to Hallie and Tim, and turned his horse around. As they cantered away, followed by the other braves, Walking Tall twisted his body to peek around his protector and give Hallie and Tim a wave and big smile.

After a shocked silence, Captain Jones boomed, "What in the name of heaven just happened?"

Hallie pulled on Tim's hand and started back toward their wagon. Cooper trotted his horse in front of her and said, "Not so fast." He glanced at Tim and dismounted. "Go back to the wagon. I need to speak with your mother alone."

"Yes, sir."

Before Hallie knew what Cooper was about, he lifted her side saddle onto the front of his horse and then mounted behind her. Holding her within the protection of his arms, he flicked the reins and turned his horse away from the wagons.

Hallie said breathlessly, "What are you doing?"

"Getting an answer to one question."

"Wh-what question?"

"Did you help that boy escape?"

"Ah…well…"

"I thought so."

"You would have done the same thing," she accused.

Cooper laughed softly. "Perhaps." Then he laughed loudly, "Sweetheart, you may have just saved the lives of everyone on our train."

Hallie glanced sharply at him and then couldn't turn away. Her mouth was only inches from his and her intent to kiss him must have been reflected on her face because his laughing ceased and he halted Sweet Pea. She was so close she could feel his chest vibrate when he spoke. "Hallie, I'll not deny there's an attraction between us, but what you've got in mind is not a good idea."

Ignoring his warning, she placed her lips on his, enjoying the fact that there was no mud getting in the way.

For a second, Cooper remained perfectly still, and then he moved his mouth gently over hers. Hallie melted against his body and clutched the front of his duster. He lingered the kiss a few seconds and then leaned back, but Hallie followed his movement. Lifting his arms to her shoulders to gently push her back and break contact, he said, "I need to get you back to your wagon. I don't think anyone saw us kiss because our backs are to them, but still, I can imagine the wagging tongues of the Pittance group just by me riding out with you."

Hallie willed herself not to cry at his rejection.

By evening of the next day, they arrived at Fort Casper.

Chapter 24: Audaciousness

At dawn of their first day camped outside Fort Casper, Hallie searched out Cooper tending the animals and her determination to apologize wavered as mortification ate its way up her body. However, her conscience wouldn't let her retreat.

Cooper heard her approach and turned. So penetrating was his gaze that she wanted to slink away and forget why she'd come. Before she lost her courage, she blurted, "Cooper, I'd like to–"

He stepped close and lifted a finger to her lips to still whatever she was about to say. "Come with me," he said low and motioned her to follow him.

Walking past their wagon, he led her to the seclusion of a copse of trees. Leaning against the trunk of one he said, "Now say what you want. I get sick of wondering whose watching and listening to everything we do."

Hallie fortified her courage. "I-I just wanted to say I'm sorry for my audacious behavior and ask that you please put the unseemly incident behind us. Well, actually, the two incidents."

Locked into his gaze, Hallie watched him break eye contact and squat to snap off a blade of grass, stick it between his teeth and from that position, lock eyes with her again. "Now what unseemly behavior might that be, Hallie?"

Hallie's eyes widened and she stammered, "M-my kissing you…yesterday and…and at the Platte River."

Cooper adjusted the blade in his mouth. "Now why would you think it was unseemly?"

Hallie couldn't believe his response and her heart tripped. "B-because it's…it's…"

Cooper quirked an eyebrow, "It's what?" Slowly, he rose off his haunches, towering above her.

Hallie's mouth went dry when he stepped to within a hairs breadth of her body. A twitch moved the corner of his mouth and he reached for the blade of grass, tossing it to the ground. Hallie's eyes widened when he continued, "I'm tired of fighting this and I was thinkin' maybe you could do a repeat and show me the audacious part."

Hallie's voice deserted her and she stood frozen like a statue.

Cooper's gaze shifted to her mouth, back to her eyes, and returned to her mouth. Softly, he whispered, "Kiss me, Hallie."

Like a moth drawn into a fire, Hallie stood on tiptoe and moved her mouth toward his at the same time he lowered his head. When their lips touched, she clutched his shoulders, hauling herself tightly against him. He smiled against her mouth and then did what she craved, kissed her without restraint. He braced the back of her head with one of his big hands and angled it just right. His tongue flicked her bottom lip and she melted against him, opening her mouth to his exploration. *Oh, sweet Jesus!*

When Cooper reached to cup her backside with his free hand and pull her tightly against his hips, she moaned and almost begged him to drop her in the grass. Releasing her grip on his shirt, she had an urge to mimic him and grab his backside, too, but courage failed her there. Instead, she wrapped her arms around his neck and mated her tongue with his.

A noise startled them and they burst apart. Hallie gathered her wits and turned to see Tim's shocked expression.

* * *

Cooper wanted to curse—loudly. Instead he stepped away from Hallie and said, "Tim, I don't want you to be upset. This wasn't your ma's doin'."

Tim moved his gaze from Cooper to his mother. In a voice choking with emotion, he said, "Pa ain't been dead long at all. How do you think he's feelin' watchin' from heaven?"

Hallie stepped forward on a soft cry, "Tim, please–"

The boy turned and ran back to camp.

Lifting a trembling hand to her lips, Hallie turned eyes overflowing with tears toward Cooper and rasped, "He's right. This is so improper."

Cooper watched Hallie retreating as she rushed after her son. He reached into his pocket and pulled out the makings for a smoke, all the while repeating every curse word he knew, even inventing some new ones.

Throughout the day, while making repairs to their wagon, he kept a close watch on Hallie and Tim. Her attempts to speak with her son were virtually ignored and she did not press him to listen; probably a good idea for now. As for her speaking to Cooper, she avoided him like a rabbit would a coyote. Before the day was over Cooper added a few more choice words to his vocabulary.

At a meeting to discuss the current "Important Particulars," Captain Jones advised the pioneers that they were at a crucial point in their travels. He warned that after leaving Fort Casper they would be crossing the North Platte at Guinard's Toll Bridge, three miles away, and the terrain would become barren, with good grazing and water in short supply. He highly suggested that anyone needing to avail themselves of the blacksmith and well-stocked trading post should not procrastinate because they were leaving the day after next.

Cooper decided to change their axle and after smashing his thumb a couple of times, was finally able to concentrate on the task at hand.

Supper was a solemn occasion. Tim received his plate from his mother and promptly walked past the animals to eat alone. Hallie dished her own plate and climbed inside her wagon.

Left alone, Cooper ladled beans over biscuits, the worst he'd ever tasted, and walked toward Tim. Immediately, the boy removed himself to another place. Cooper sighed and wished he didn't feel such longing for Hallie.

Chapter 25: Reconciliation at Independence Rock

Hallie walked beside her wagon as it rolled toward the toll bridge spanning the North Platte. Before breaking camp that morning, Captain Jones had ordered that lots be cast to determine the order of the wagons for travel, and hers had come in next to last. Ahead of her, the Pittance schooner was about to cross over, with Mrs. Pittance haggling the price of the toll. It was then that Pastor Pittance stepped beside his wife and handed the operator the amount he'd asked for. Although Mrs. Pittance's face contorted in anger, she did not argue.

When Cooper led Hallie's wagon forward, she moved to pay the Frenchman, but Cooper reached into his pocket, selected some coins, and paid the toll. Unreasonable anger lodged in Hallie's heart. She determined that as soon as they were on the other side, she would reimburse the amount to him.

When they had crossed over, she confronted Cooper. "How much do I owe you?"

"Nothing."

"That's ridiculous. How much do I owe you?"

Cooper settled piercing blue eyes on hers and stubbornly repeated, "Nothing."

Hallie tried again. "Cooper, I will not let you spend your money on my expenses."

His eyes flashed. "Hallie, you can argue until hell freezes, but I paid the toll; end of story." He motioned behind her. "Maybe you can help him."

Hallie turned to see Stubby and his small cart pulled by one ox turning his load around. She frowned and turned back to Cooper. He shrugged.

Redirecting her exasperation from Cooper to Stubby, she stalked back across the bridge and called to the toll operator, "Excuse me. Why is he turning around?"

"Enchanté," the little man said, and then in accented English, "He requires more money to cross my bridge. I told him to go sell something and return."

Hallie watched Stubby's dejected posture as he steered his ox back toward the fort. Sighing, she said, "I'll pay his toll. How much?"

The Frenchman grinned, shouted at Stubby, and reached his hand out for her money. He said, "I am a fair man. I never charge the same for carts as big wagons."

After paying the price that was, indeed, fair, Hallie rushed back across the bridge. As soon as she reached her wagon, Cooper cracked the whip and the animals moved forward. She sighed, glad Tim was with the Hankersons and couldn't feel the animosity she was harboring toward Cooper.

As Captain Jones had warned, travel became even more difficult and the ground yielded little in the way of grass for the animals or good streams for water. After several days and fifty miserable miles, with dust so thick at times they had to wear kerchiefs over their mouths, a shout passed from wagon to wagon, "Independence Rock!"

Hallie stepped away from her wagon and smiled her first real smile in days. And when Tim, following her, returned her smile, the landmark was forgotten and a tear slipped down her cheek. Perhaps her son had forgiven her behavior. She opened her arms. He hesitated and then stepped into the circle of her hug. Leaning over and holding her boy tightly, she said, "I'm so sorry, Tim. Please forgive me."

Tim sniffed, "No, Ma. I'm sorry. I shouldn't have–"

"Don't say anything, son. You were right. Your pa's only been dead a few months. I don't know what I was thinking."

"But, ma–"

"We won't talk about it anymore. Let's just think about our place in Oregon." She pointed toward Independence Rock. "Son, that rock is another milestone on our journey. Captain Jones said that beyond it is the Sweetwater River."

Independence Rock was reached in the late afternoon, and even though there was still daylight for travel, Captain Jones called camp. A few adventurous pioneers climbed to the top of the rock and came back with stories of hundreds of names scrawled on it, testament to previous travelers. They also said they saw sweeping views of the Sweetwater River, the river that would guide them to Devil's Gate and South Pass. The spirit of the camp soared and that night a celebration broke out with music; they were almost halfway to Oregon!

Hallie watched Tim playing with a group of boys and sniffed back another wave of melancholy. Her relationship with her son was healed, but feelings for Cooper persisted. Searching the camp she saw him speaking with the fancy ladies. A lump lodged in her throat while longing lodged in her heart. When he laughed at something Clarissa said, Hallie had to look away to battle her jealousy. Hallie's friendship with Clarissa had deepened and guilt plagued her for jealousy over a man she needed to purge from her heart.

A familiar voice interrupted her conflicting emotions. "Ma'am?"

Hallie turned to see Stubby standing with his hat in hand. "Yes, Stubby."

"Seems I owe you again. I been gettin' the courage up to thank you fer the loan at the bridge. I'll repay–"

"It wasn't a loan. You don't have to repay me."

Stubby turned scarlet. "That's where you're wrong, ma'am. I'll pay you back, that's fer sure."

Hallie said, "This is probably none of my business, but I once heard you say you had done well with the cards. What happened to–"

Stubby turned even redder. "Me 'n Harley lost almost ever-thing in a card game at Fort Kearney."

Trying to keep the censor out of her voice, Hallie said, "Well, it's time to put the past behind you and look to the future. You can't change what's already happened." She knew she was speaking the words as much to herself as to Stubby.

The fiddlers tapped the count to another tune and Sharon interrupted them. "Stubby, how 'bout a dance?"

Hallie glanced from Stubby to Sharon and saw jealousy in her eyes. *Are you kidding me?* Quickly, she said, "Gotta go find my son."

* * *

The following day, Captain Jones led the wagons south of a chasm carved by the Sweetwater River and aptly named Devil's Gate because of its jagged granite rocks.

Once past the gorge, the Captain halted the wagons and ordered Cooper and several other men to go in search of the pronghorn that populated the area.

Cooper and the men returned with three kills and camp was called so the animals could be cleaned and cooked. That night everyone enjoyed fresh meat.

While Cooper sat beside the fire and filled himself with the delicious meal, he watched Hallie speaking with Clarissa. As unlikely as it seemed, a prostitute and a farm girl had formed a bond of friendship. He continued to watch Hallie and gulped a mouthful of hot coffee that burned the hell out of his tongue. *Damn, I've got to get my mind off Hallie.*

Hallie turned from speaking with Clarissa, met his gaze, and quickly looked away. Even so, the eye contact was enough to scorch the air.

Cooper cursed again and looked to where Tim was warming himself beside Emmett and Lydia's campfire. Chewing another bite of pronghorn, he wondered how he could restore his relationship with the boy. Like his mother, Tim avoided him, although sometimes he caught the kid watching him and wondered what he was thinking. All-in-all, Cooper was feeling pretty low down and didn't know how to make things right.

Chapter 26: Parting of the Waters and Parting of the Ways

Following the Sweetwater River the wagons entered South Pass, the only way through the Rocky Mountains. Surprisingly, the wide passage stretching for miles in every direction ascended so gradually as to almost not be recognized as an ascent. At the crest, Captain Jones halted the train and trotted Midnight the length, shouting, "It may not look like much, but we're at the Continental Divide where the waters part and run in opposite directions. We're also over halfway to our destination."

A shout arose among the emigrants. Hallie and Tim held hands and circled in a happy dance. For an instant, Hallie smiled lovingly at Cooper and his breath caught. He wanted to join the dance with them.

* * *

The day after crossing the Continental Divide the group reached the Parting of the Ways, a crossroad where the train in front of them turned off. Unexpectedly, some of the wagons in their own group pulled into the open field to bypass their fellow travelers and hitch up with the other train.

Confused, Hallie asked Cooper, "What are they doing?"

Cooper explained. "Some of our folks got to conversing with the other train and learned that once they reached Parting of the Ways there was another road called the Sublette Route that would save about forty miles, and they decided to hitch up with them."

"Hmm. There must be a reason Captain Jones isn't choosing to go that direction."

"There sure is. It bypasses Fort Bridger and crosses the Little Colorado Desert without water for fifty miles."

Hallie frowned. "I wish them all the best, but I trust Captain Jones's judgment."

Cooper pushed his Stetson back. "At least only four wagons were persuaded to leave our train."

A week later, Captain Jones called camp outside Fort Bridger. Hallie said to Tim, "We're on the downward side of our journey and I think we should celebrate with a treat."

Tim looked at his mother expectantly.

Hallie winked. "Surely, the trading post has candy."

He grinned. "I hope they have licorice."

When Cooper walked toward the fort, Hallie and Tim joined him. Cooper said, "Later, we need to inventory our supplies and tomorrow I'll bring the wagon into the fort to stock up."

Hallie pointed to the south. "What is that mountain range?"

"Those are the Uinta Mountains."

She inhaled deeply. "The sky is so blue here and the air so fresh."

The trading post proved to be one of the best so far. As promised, Hallie bought candy for Tim, and unknown to him, she purchased extra licorice to surprise him with later down the road.

That night, while Hallie sat around her campfire and enjoyed a licorice stick herself, she suddenly realized she hadn't seen Prudence Pittance for a day or so. Glancing in the direction of Pastor and Mrs. Pittance's wagon, she watched a woman enter carrying a tray of food.

The next day, after setting out on their journey, Hallie walked alongside Clarissa to pass the monotony of plodding along.

Hallie said, "I haven't seen Pastor or Mrs. Pittance lately. Have you?"

Clarissa brushed back a stray strand of fiery red hair and turned to look at her. "I think the pastor is ill. I heard one of the women in their congregation telling Captain Jones he was feeling a might poorly."

"When was that?"

"It was the day we reached Fort Bridger."

"Well, even though they're not my favorite people, I certainly hope it's nothing serious."

"I agree. I don't like them much either, but I'm not so mean as to wish anything bad on them."

Changing the subject, Hallie said, "I heard Captain Jones telling Cooper we're going to reach Thomas Fork soon and ford another stream. He said two bridges are there now, but before they were built in the fifties, crossing was most treacherous. I'm amazed at what the emigrants before us accomplished. We have it easy compared to them."

Clarissa kicked a rock. "I suppose there will be another toll. I sure hope we don't have to pay too many more, what with havin' to buy supplies and such. A wagon train ain't the best place to earn a livin' and me and the gals are havin' to make our money stretch. Course we been servicin' the soldiers at the forts, but they can't pay the kind of money we're used to makin'."

Hallie coughed and didn't respond. Should she commiserate with Clarissa's predicament or encourage her to find another "occupation"?

Changing the subject again, she said, "Stubby and Sharon seem to be getting along well."

Clarissa laughed and said conspiratorially, "That's fer sure. We been teasin' Sharon 'bout her bein' sweet on him." She cocked her head to the side. "As fer yerself, I been noticin' that you and Cooper don't talk much. After the day he pulled you on his horse and rode off with you, I thought fer sure we'd be havin' a wedding. You know, Pastor Pittance could marry you two."

Hallie glanced sharply at Clarissa. "Cooper is simply accompanying Tim and me to Oregon. There is nothing between us."

Clarissa only raised her eyebrows and cast a doubtful look at Hallie.

Late that afternoon, Thomas Fork was reached and the creek forded over a bridge.

The next day they arrived at Big Hill and their travel became tedious as the wagons ascended the hill. The descent was even worse. Except for the usual mechanical problems with the wagons and a horse that stumbled, broke a leg, and had to be put down, they finally made it safely to Clover Creek on the other side.

Chapter 27: Sad Times at Clover Creek

Exhausted, Hallie and Tim prepared supper while Cooper tended to their animals. Only one chicken remained from the last batch they'd bought at Fort Casper and it would probably become supper within a few days. Hallie pulled a pot of rice off the fire and ladled beans over the top. She told Tim to let Cooper know supper was ready and then she lifted the Dutch oven with the cornbread onto the multifunctional wagon tailgate.

A noise across the campground captured her attention. Hallie turned to see a woman exit the back of Pastor Pittance's wagon with her hand held to her mouth, apparently trying to keep from sobbing. The men and women standing outside of the wagon all had somber expressions. *Something is definitely wrong. Maybe I should offer them supper.*

While Hallie was trying to determine if she should interfere, Sarah Jackson, the woman in the group who had first introduced herself to Hallie, stepped away from the wagon and crossed the camp toward her. Surprised, Hallie greeted her. "Hello Sarah, I heard the pastor is ill. Is there anything I can do?"

Sarah said, "He wants to see you."

Dumbfounded, Hallie replied, "He does? Why would he want to see me?"

"I don't know, but..." her voice cracked, "he's near death."

"No!" Hallie gasped.

Sarah nodded. "Will you please come?"

"Of course; but what about Mrs. Pittance?"

"She's with him and doesn't understand either. But it's his last wish."

"I'll come right now." Hallie followed Sarah to the Pittance wagon, her heart hammering with dread. Was she going to be damned for her traveling arrangement with Cooper? Pausing to inhale a calming breath, she allowed one of the men to help her into the wagon.

Pastor Pittance, a big man, appeared to have shrunk considerably. His sunken eyes were ringed with dark circles, and his breathing was the rattle before death. Sitting on the floor beside him, Mrs. Pittance held one of his hands in her own and when Hallie entered the wagon, she lifted tear-drenched eyes and motioned with her other hand to a stool at the end of his pallet for Hallie.

Softly, Mrs. Pittance said, "Husband, Mrs. Wells is here like you requested."

With great effort, the pastor lifted his eyelids and focused on Hallie. A weak smile creased the corners of his mouth. He said, "Thank you…for coming." With a barely perceptible motion of his free hand, he continued, "This old ticker has been giving me trouble for a long time."

Mrs. Pittance sniffed loudly, looked at Hallie, and said, "I didn't know."

Pastor Pittance shifted his gaze to his wife and rasped, "I didn't let you know."

Tears stung Hallie's eyes and she said, "What is it that I can do for you, Pastor Pittance?"

He returned his gaze back to Hallie. "Comfort my wife after my death. She isn't the woman you think she is."

Mrs. Pittance sobbed in earnest. "Don't leave me, husband."

Tears dripped down Halley cheeks at the scene.

Fixing his eyes on his wife with an expression of love and tenderness, Pastor Pittance said, "You know I forgave you long ago, don't you?" With great effort he inhaled and continued in a whisper, "And I loved those girls like my own."

Mrs. Pittance sobbed softly.

Pastor Pittance moved his free hand toward his wife. "Grasp my hand, wife."

Mrs. Pittance gently clutched his hand. His voice was now stronger. "After the girls died, you changed. I know you believed you were doing good by becoming so upstanding and wanting everyone to follow your lead, but it's time to stop. I've never believed in interfering with the work the Good Lord does in one's heart, and he's been working mightily on you these past three years since their deaths, but now that I'm about to pass on, you will become the leader of our flock."

Mrs. Pittance sobbed, "No, husband, no. I am not worthy."

Hallie saw the pastor barely squeeze his wife's hands and, ignoring her cry to the contrary said, "You will be worthy after the Lord finishes his work in you through Hallie."

Hallie gasped.

With tears overflowing, Mrs. Pittance said, "No, I cannot–"

Struggling to breathe Pastor Pittance wheezed, "I love you, wife, but now it's time for me to join Clara and Ella, and it's time for you to expand your heart and accept others unconditionally."

Hallie watched the quiet pastor turn his gaze upward and his demeanor change from one of pain to serenity. He mouthed the words, "Clara, Ella," and with an imperceptible smile, slipped gently into death.

Mrs. Pittance let out a wail and threw herself on her husband's chest. Having lost her own husband only a few months earlier, Hallie reached to touch her shoulder. Compassion swelled her heart. "It will always hurt, but it will become bearable."

Clutching her husband's shoulders, Mrs. Pittance sobbed. "You don't understand!" She wept several minutes and then confessed her sin. "I was unfaithful to my husband but he loved me anyway; even when I bore twin daughters that were not his." She sobbed again. "They both died of the cholera at age twelve and I knew it was God's way of punishing me. Since then, I've tried to atone for my mistake by being as pure as I can be and leading others on the same path." She lifted a face streaked with tears. "But I failed. I failed my husband, my girls, my congregation...I failed myself."

The back flap of the wagon lifted and from the expressions on those gathered, they had heard Mrs. Pittance's heartrending confession. Hallie moved to the opening and announced, "Pastor Pittance left the care of his flock to his wife and he would not have done so had he not believed in her. As you have undoubtedly heard, she has suffered terribly. And you have all been given an opportunity to either increase her suffering or comfort her. What would the Good Lord have you do?"

Beyond the crowd, Hallie saw Tim standing beside Cooper. Cooper said, "Excuse me, please." Stepping forward, he lifted Hallie from the wagon and placed his arm around her shoulders to lead her back to their wagon.

The next afternoon, amidst many tears, Pastor Pittance was laid to rest at Clover Creek with the words, "Beloved Husband, Father, and Pastor," crudely etched into the rock that would stand guard over his grave. Mrs. Pittance, her face ragged with sorrow, was surrounded by a compassionate congregation.

Chapter 28: Heart to Heart at Shoshone Falls

A contemplative atmosphere hovered over the wagons as they departed Clover Creek and headed toward their next notable landmark. During the two days it took to reach Soda Springs, Hallie didn't see Mrs. Pittance. However, she was heartened to see members of her church often entering her wagon.

Everyone's mood lightened when they camped at the springs. Captain Jones said it was one of the major attractions on the Oregon Trail, and Hallie could certainly understand why, with hot springs and erupting geysers marking the landscape. The emigrants captured the water in barrels, marveling over its wonderful taste. According to the captain more than one hundred springs dotted the area.

Hallie laughed when several of the emigrants cheerfully announced that the water was quite stimulating, producing an almost intoxicating effect if imbibed in abundance.

At their evening gathering Captain Jones announced, "Although I don't encourage it, I have an obligation to let ya'll know that a few miles away is the Hudspeth's Cutoff that heads toward California. If anyone has a mind to go in that direction, I'll draw a map and tell ya everything I know about it, but like I said, I don't encourage anyone to leave the group; leastwise not by themselves. So, is anyone thinkin' 'bout turnin' toward Cali?"

There was a murmuring among the gathering, but no one voiced any intent to leave the train.

Captain Jones smiled. "Good. Now movin' on to other matters, in a few days we'll reach Fort Hall and replenish supplies as best we can. Unless the fort has changed, it's not very well stocked. However, this would be a good time to make sure your wagons are in top condition. We've traveled a long ways and they've takin' a beating. Your wagon breakin' down on the trail, when it's something you could have averted with common sense, not only hinders you, but everyone else."

A couple of days later, with the whitewashed walls of Fort Hall glistening in the distance, everyone picked up the pace, anxious to meet other folks from other trains and compare experiences. Many of the emigrants kept diaries, including Hallie, who had jotted her experiences to be relived throughout the years.

A voice behind her startled her. "Mrs. Wells, may I speak with you?" It was Mrs. Pittance.

Hallie turned and said, "Of course."

She glanced at Tim, who said without her prompting, "Can I go visit with the Livermans' boys?"

"Yes. But don't stay more than an hour."

"Okay, Ma."

Cooper turned at the sound of Mrs. Pittance's voice, but merely nodded a greeting and turned back around.

Mrs. Pittance kept pace with Hallie for several minutes before speaking, a tremor in her voice, "My husband's death was a complete surprise and it…it made me rethink my life and purpose."

Hallie glanced sideways at the contrite woman and marveled at the change in her attitude. She probably hadn't reached the age of fifty, and whereas she had appeared much older when Hallie first met her, she now appeared much younger. The disapproving scowl was gone and with her face relaxed and her hair combed less severely, she was almost pretty. In fact, Hallie would bet her bottom dollar that the woman had once been a beauty. Rather than reply, she waited for Mrs. Pittance to continue.

"I know that I can never repay you for the kindness you have shown me, but I want to tell you how sorry I am for treating you the way I did. Y-you heard my confession of sin, but if the truth be told, I will never regret the birth of my girls. Pastor Pittance and I were childless, and after the girls came, he forgave me and loved them like his own." She inhaled a ragged breath. "We actually became a happy family, but when the girls died within days of each other, I believed it was punishment for my act of weakness with a drifter just passing through our community." She hesitated and finished with, "And a sweet-talker. I never saw him again and he never knew about his daughters."

Several minutes passed before Mrs. Pittance continued. "Anyway, you heard what the pastor said about me trying to make everyone sinless. I figured it was my calling…but I was wrong. Seeing your kindness to others has shown me that." A little sob escaped. "It took my dear husband's death to make me see the truth."

Hallie reached to hold Mrs. Pittance's hand and asked, "May I call you Prudence?"

The sad woman nodded through tears.

"And you must call me Hallie."

"Thank you, Hallie."

Thus began a newfound friendship.

* * *

Captain Jones pressed the emigrants to continue forward at a more rapid pace and finally Fort Hall was reached. The tired group did little more than prepare supper and care for their animals before falling exhausted into bed.

The next morning Cooper escorted Hallie and Tim to the reality of Fort Hall, a rather pitiful encampment with scanty supplies. The only bright spot was that emigrants from two other trains were also there. Soon folks were mingling and sharing stories.

Cooper lazed against the outside wall of the blacksmith's, watching the goings-on around him while having work done on some wagon parts. Across the road, Hallie was engaged in animated conversation with a young woman holding a baby, and when the woman handed the baby to Hallie, Cooper inhaled sharply at the expression on her face. She definitely needed more children, and when an unguarded thought escaped that he should be the father of those children, he literally shook his head to dislodge the idea.

With his gaze still on Hallie, he watched her lift the baby to kiss its cheek and her eyes met his. Quickly, she looked away, but not before he saw her longing. His heart also burned with desire and he knew the attraction between them was not going to disappear. The sooner they arrived in Oregon and he got her settled, the sooner he could leave. An Oregonian farmer would probably have her married and bedded before another year passed. The thought of another man bedding Hallie and being the recipient of her kisses and caresses made him groan. It seemed no matter the direction of his thoughts, they always returned to her.

* * *

Whereas the train had followed Bear River up to Soda Springs, after leaving Fort Hall they followed the Snake River. Captain Jones said they would soon reach a landmark called Gate of Death, a narrow passage through massive rocks. He alerted the pioneers to the fact that there were occasional skirmishes with Indians in the area and that a deadly one had erupted in 1862. Although an encounter was unlikely, he advised everyone to stay alert and keep their guns handy. A tense atmosphere hovered until they had traveled well beyond the area.

They reached the next trading post, Rock Creek Stage Station, ten days after leaving Fort Hall. Being an intersection for a stage route and another trail, the Kelton Road from Utah, the post proved to be well stocked. After their exhausting journey across the parched Snake River Plain, the abundant water and grass at the station brightened everyone's spirits.

Captain Jones announced that they'd be staying at this stop longer than he'd first intended so man and beast could recoup before beginning the next leg of their journey. On the third day, much conversation buzzed about a marvelous site residents of the fort described as the Niagara Falls of the West—Shoshone Falls. When a group decided to trek the few miles to the falls, Hallie wanted to join them, and when Cooper said, "Come on, get Tim, and let's go," she didn't hesitate.

That is, until she realized their only horse was Sweet Pea."

Cooper seemed to read her mind. "You and Tim will ride Sweet Pea while I guide her."

"Then we must take turns so you don't have to walk the entire way."

Cooper only smiled and Hallie knew he would be a gentleman and not allow her to walk. Not surprising, the five miles to the falls seemed minuscule compared to what they had accomplished over the past weeks.

Long before they reached the falls, a roar of such magnitude arose that the emigrants nervously eyed each other.

Hallie's first sight of the cascading water literally took her breath away and Tim, seated behind her on Sweet Pea, said, "Oh, Ma, I never thought to see the likes of anything so grand in my life."

From a safe vantage point, the twenty emigrants who had banded together to travel to the falls, dismounted their horses, laid out blankets, and unpacked lunches. Tim joined up with the Liverman boys playing tag and climbing trees.

Hallie sat alone on her blanket and unpacked hardtack and fried chicken and surprised Cooper with some dried fruit. He accepted the plate she handed him and returned to the tree he had been leaning against. She nibbled a piece of apricot because her stomach was flip-flopping at being alone with Cooper. From beneath her lashes, she saw him watching her. The expression he wore was so sad it made her frown. After a moment's hesitation, she summoned her courage and said, "You had another nightmare last night, didn't you?"

"I'm sorry I woke you."

She fingered a fold on the blanket. "I was about to wake you, but you got up and walked out of camp."

Cooper didn't respond, but kept looking at her.

Summoning more courage she said, "I want to relate something Tim said shortly after we left the Shawnee Mission."

"Okay."

Hallie's heart pounded so hard she wondered if Cooper could see the pulse in her neck. "He told me that when he talks to me about his father's death, he feels better." She inhaled slowly to calm herself. "He said that he sees sadness in your eyes and he thinks that if you talked about whatever it is that's bothering you, maybe you would feel better, too."

Unable to meet Cooper's gaze, Hallie studied the fold in the blanket. Finally, the suspense was so unbearable she lifted her eyes to his. He watched her with an intensity that took her breath away. Her heart pounded at her boldness.

Cooper shifted his gaze to the sky, the same color as his eyes, and then back to her. "I have a fifteen-year-old son whom I haven't seen since he was three."

Hallie waited and prayed that he would continue.

"I told you once that I was married and divorced. Well, the child was born from that marriage. My wife was a good woman, but she longed for what I couldn't give her—family life. During our marriage, I was absent more than I was present. I had the run in me." He shifted his stance to pull out a smoke and Hallie continued to play with the fold in the blankct while he rolled it.

He struck his match on his boot and lit his cigarette. "I found my wife in bed with the local banker and almost killed them both."

It took all of Hallie's willpower not to gasp, although her eyes widened.

"At the last minute, I realized what a sorry-ass excuse for a man I was and gave her what she'd wanted for over a year—a divorce."

Hallie attempted to speak, but her voice cracked. She tried again. "Twelve years is a long time. Maybe your boy wants to see you as much as you want to see him."

"And maybe he doesn't. Maybe he never wants to see me."

"But you'll never know if you don't try."

Cooper blew smoke into the air. "I don't have the courage to see him or my ex-wife."

"I don't believe that."

A slight smile creased Cooper's face. "You know I want to bed you, don't you?"

Hallie's eyes rounded at the change in their conversation.

Cooper took a draw on his cigarette and then released the smoke. "There's an attraction between us that we both keep denying."

Rather than acknowledge the truth of what he'd said, Hallie slid her gaze from his.

"Hallie, I'm not the marrying kind. If I was, I'd make you my wife in a heartbeat."

She swallowed against the lump in her throat.

Cooper said tenderly, "Like I promised, I won't act on my desires. You're an honorable woman and you deserve an honorable husband. In fact, if I was a betting man, and I once was, I'd bet you're married to a fine gentleman within a year or two."

Cooper tossed his cigarette and stepped on it. Gazing back at her, he said, "I'm just not that man."

Chapter 29: Showdown at Fort Boise

Hallie walked beside Mrs. Pittance as they traveled toward Thousand Springs, a place Captain Jones assured the emigrants they would never forget. They caught up with the Snake River again and followed the winding trail as it turned north, west, and then north again.

Hallie had discovered a wonderful friend in Mrs. Pittance and wished it hadn't taken the death of Pastor Pittance to breathe new life into the woman. She sighed, resigning herself to the fact that life was sometimes discovered in death.

Mrs. Pittance said, "Hallie, are you feeling all right? You haven't seemed yourself for several days."

Hallie wanted to confide in Prudence, but confessing her feelings for Cooper would only entrench her heartbreak more deeply.

"I'm fine. I think I'm just succumbing to the walking blues." She chuckled. "We've only been walking for three months."

Prudence patted her hand. "Dear, maybe you should stop fighting your feelings for Cooper."

Hallie fingered a tear. "I try and I try, but what Clarissa told me once is so true—the heart does what the heart wants. Besides, he's made it clear that as soon as he has me and Tim settled in Oregon, he's returning to Missouri." Hallie's voice caught on a little sob, "And I'll never see him again."

Prudence placed her arm around Hallie's shoulder. "Honey, as sure as I am that the Good Lord hears our prayers, I know that Cooper has feelings for you."

Hallie glanced a few wagons ahead at Cooper leading the oxen and felt such love her heart wanted to burst. No longer did she silently apologize to her dead husband for loving another man. The love she felt for Cooper could never be wrong.

After a few more descending zigzags in the trail, Thousand Springs came into view. The phenomenal vista of water gushing from black rocks seemed surreal. For a moment, Hallie forgot her heartache as she absorbed the scene. It was as if everything good and beautiful and honorable existed in those fleeting seconds, and when Cooper turned around and met her gaze, even at a distance, that goodness, beauty, and honorableness became a living thing between them.

After he turned back around, Prudence leaned in and whispered, "He loves you, Hallie."

The rest of the day was spent traveling through what Captain Jones said was the Hagerman Valley, a place of pristine beauty.

The next day, Captain Jones led them to an area called Three Island Ford and called his leaders together. After an hour's meeting, the men returned to their designated sections of the train and explained what Captain Jones had decided would be best.

To the group gathered around him, Cooper said, "We're going to ford the river here because the water is low and we'll save time. If the water were high, we'd be forced to continue along the trail to another crossing upstream, but Captain Jones says it's more difficult there. After we leave the river we'll cross some more plains, and then we'll enter the beautiful Boise River Valley where Fort Boise is located." He winked. "And we're going to see trees again."

Although the emigrants appeared apprehensive about the river crossing, his last statement brought smiles to everyone.

Clarissa said, "What I wouldn't give to lay under the shade of a tree."

One of the Liverman boys called out, "And I want to climb one."

After a few more comments that lightened the atmosphere, Cooper gave instructions for preparing for the crossing. Whereas most of their crossings had been by ferry or bridge, or easily accomplished on small streams, this one would be their most daunting.

Before the group disbanded to attend to their wagons, Cooper said, "Now ya'll know after traveling with me that I'm a cautious man. I'm hopin' my words will comfort you. The water's not so deep that we have to lash the wagons together or swim the animals across. The river's wide, I'll grant you that, but we'll make it over just fine."

Cooper's smile and words of encouragement were just what the pioneers needed and spirits lifted.

As the first wagons began crossing with Captain Jones in the lead, the water reached high on the wheels and even floated some wagon beds. But the pioneers, having traveled so far, faced the task of fording the river with courage and determination.

Under the sharp tongue of Mrs. Pittance, Stubby's cart was lashed to her own wagon to ensure its safe crossing. Walking alongside Mrs. Pittance's oxen, and up to his chest in water, Stubby appeared more fearful of the preacher woman than he did of the deepening river as she sang high praises to the Lord from her perch.

Standing on the bank, Hallie laughed at the sight. Prudence seemed determined to make Stubby a believer.

Before the day was over, all the wagons had crossed the Snake River and a shout arose among the pioneers.

At Bonneville Point three days later, an even greater shout arose than the one after crossing the river, for a verdant valley lay before them with trees!

Two days after that they camped beside the Boise River and Captain Jones boomed at their meeting, "Folks, we're over fourteen hundred miles from Westport! That's almost three quarters of the way to Oregon!

* * *

Cooper kicked back with Captain Jones and Emmett at a saloon in Fort Boise and listened to an old-timer share the fort's history with anyone who would listen. Seems this was the latter of two forts with the same name. The first one, fifty miles northwest, had been pioneered in the 1830s by the Hudson's Bay Company and abandoned in the 1850s. This newest fort built by the Union Army during the War of the States boasted a sawmill, lime kiln, and sandstone quarry. The fort's location was outstanding for water, grass, wood, and stone. In fact, it was a popular place for travel weary emigrants to stay and make their homes there.

Captain Jones confirmed this. "This is a right nice place and some of the families in our train have let me know they'll not be movin' on."

Cooper was curious. "Which families might that be?"

"The Ludlows, for one, and the McAllisters, for another. I kinda got my suspicion that a few more might join them."

Cooper glanced at Emmett. "How about you?"

Emmett said, "As beautiful as it is, Lydia and I have our hearts set on the Willamette Valley."

Captain Jones grinned and asked, "Well, Emmett, since I'm losing two of my leaders, how would you like to volunteer for the position. Saves me havin' to appoint you."

Emmett gave the captain a speculative look, reminding Cooper of a juror weighing a verdict, and asked seriously, "Do you think I have what it takes?"

Captain Jones glanced at Cooper. "Well, Coop? Does Emmett have what it takes?"

Cooper frowned as if pondering a deep question and then, suddenly smiling, said, "I surely do."

Relief washed over Emmett's face. Captain Jones said, "Since we all gave up whiskey years ago, how 'bout we celebrate with some more sarsaparillas?"

Cooper and Emmett lifted their glasses and said, "Hear, hear!"

A pretty saloon gal delivered a round of sarsaparillas and Captain Jones lifted his mug. "Damn, I miss the whisky."

Again, Cooper and Emmett agreed. "Hear, hear!"

For the next hour the men enjoyed jovial conversation and praised a journey that had only seen the death of two men, four mules, a few oxen, three horses, two cows, and all of the chickens. They laughed over the latter. Emmett said, "My Lydia makes the best fried chicken I ever tasted."

Cooper said, "I have to agree with you there." He swigged the last of his drink. "Guess I best get back and check my animals."

Captain Jones and Emmett concurred and started to push away from the table when scuffling across the room and shouting got everyone's attention. "Get the hell out of my way!"

The three of them looked up to see a tall man who obviously hadn't bathed in days—maybe weeks—with a salt and pepper straggly beard, matted hair, and wild eyes, pointing at Emmett. Still sitting at the table, Cooper edged his hand toward his revolver.

The wild man said, "Move your hand again and you're a dead man." Then with his hand poised over his own gun he said to Emmett, "Stand up, Cheyenne Jack. I'd know your face anywhere. You killed my brother in a gunfight and now I'm gonna kill you."

Cooper said calmly, "You're obviously mistaken, sir. Why don't you join us while we figure this out?"

Without moving his gaze to Cooper, the gunfighter said, "Shut yer mouth!"

Emmett, who had thus far been silent, slowly rose with his hands extended, palms up. "I'll handle this."

Patrons of the saloon had removed themselves to the edges of the room and suddenly made haste toward the swinging doors.

Captain Jones said low, "Cooper, Cheyenne Jack is well able to handle this."

Cooper's gaze shot to Emmett, who nodded his agreement, and he felt like he'd been gut kicked. Mild-mannered Emmett was legendary lawman Cheyenne Jack, who supposedly died in a cholera epidemic back in the late fifties?

Emmett pushed his chair back with his foot. To his accuser, he said, "Sir, if you would like to know the truth of what happened I would be happy to explain."

The man's face contorted in rage and he snarled, "You bushwhacked my brother!"

Calmly, Emmett responded, "No, sir. You have it backward. Your brother bushwhacked me."

The man sputtered some profanities and Emmett said, "I don't want to kill you. Like my friend said, why don't you join us and we'll talk this out."

With a crazed expression, the cowboy went for his gun. Before it was barely out of its holster, Emmett shot the man dead center between his eyes with the gun Cooper knew he kept strapped inside his jacket above his waist.

Silence filled the saloon, and then men began rushing back through the doors. Those who had heard of the famous Texas lawman stared at Emmett in admiration. Cooper was still trying to process the revelation when the captain of the fort and several military men burst in. Emmett dropped his gun on the table, raised his hands above his head, and said, "I'm ready for you to take me in for questioning."

* * *

After an hour-long interrogation, Commander Rickert released Emmett to be reunited with his tearful wife. Captain Jones had given his statement earlier, along with the eyewitnesses, and returned to camp shortly thereafter. Cooper now walked back to camp with Emmett, Lydia, and Hallie, who had stayed with Lydia to offer support.

Emmett said, "I guess I owe ya'll an explanation."

Lydia sniffed and Emmett wrapped his arm around her shoulders. "My ma and pa had eight boys and I was the youngest. My given name is Charles Jack, but my eldest brother nicknamed me Cheyenne. He said I was as red as an Indian after I was born. Anyway, we lived on a small cattle ranch and I learned young to fend for myself. My brothers taught me how to rope, shoot, wield a knife. They were all big, tough cowboys and they always gave me a hard time because of my size and studious look. They said if I didn't know how to defend myself, I'd always be recovering from beatings. My family wasn't perfect, but they weren't criminals. When I was seventeen, my ma sent me to town to pick up something for her and when I returned..." He paused, took a deep breath and said, "My family was dead; even my ma. They'd been ambushed."

Lydia gasped and Hallie let out a little cry.

Cooper said, "You don't have to talk about this if you don't want to."

Emmett sighed. "It's okay. I came to terms with my loss years ago." He paused again before saying, "It seems my eldest brother, Joe, had tangled with the wrong man. He got in a card game with a young buck and won everything. When the loser accused my brother of cheating and then jumped him outside the saloon, my brother beat him up bad. Like I said, my family wasn't perfect. Anyway, the young man ended up going blind. He was just shy of turning twenty and his father, a wealthy rancher, brought charges against Joe that were dismissed because witnesses said the boy started the fight."

The group slowed their progress as they approached the circle of wagons and Emmett lowered his voice. "Anyway, the boy killed himself. Shot himself in the head and his pa found him."

Other than Lydia sniffling, no one said anything until Cooper asked, "So the father took revenge on your family?"

"Yeah. I won't go into the particulars, but he hired killers to shoot them all. After I found out who'd done it, I went crazy and swore I'd find them and exact revenge. I told the sheriff my intent. He tried to talk me out of it, but when he couldn't, he offered an alternative. He said he'd swear me in as a deputy if I promised to let another lawman know when I'd located them so they could be brought to trial." Emmett chortled, "I wasn't fooled. The men were already wanted for heinous crimes and the sheriff knew I wouldn't be deterred in killing them. He was offering me a way to eliminate evil men without going to prison. Course, he figured they'd kill me first."

Emmett stopped walking. "It took three years but I finally found them. Originally, there were five men, but three were already dead by the time I met up with the other two. The leader was still alive and I called him out on the street of some no-name town. When I told him who I was and that I was bringing him in, he just laughed and pulled his pistol. I was faster. His companion ran out of the saloon and I shot him, too.

"After that, I showed my badge to the drunken sheriff of the town and he wanted to pin a medal on me for ridding his town of these monsters."

Emmett started walking again and stopped outside his wagon. "When I returned to my hometown and tried to give the sheriff back my badge, he asked if I wanted to become a bounty hunter. I had no family and no aspirations, so I agreed. I guess you could say the rest is history. When I started making a name for myself, I suddenly saw my life laid out before me. I would die in some dusty town at the hand of some lowlife wanting to make a name for himself. While I was trying to figure out how to disappear and start over I got the cholera. Most of the town got it and most of them died. I figured I'd die, too, but when I started to recover, I told the sheriff that I wanted to start over as someone else and he went along with it. Since the cholera hadn't killed me, he said it was a sign from God that he should help me.

"There were so many dying that when he added my name to the list, no one questioned him. I hid out in an abandoned shack and when I was able, rode out and never looked back. I changed my appearance from scraggly to what you see now." He chuckled. "My hair started receding early on and aided my disguise. I left Texas, got a new name, and visited several states, ending up in Missouri, where I met Lydia."

He pulled his wife into an embrace. "I'm so sorry for not telling you, sweetheart, but I just couldn't take a chance on losing you, and when Sam was born, I felt such joy…" His voice cracked and Lydia lifted her arms to encircle his neck.

She said, "I'll always be here for you, Emmett."

After returning Lydia's embrace and kissing her forehead, Emmett stepped back and said, "Contrary to what I told you before, I was good at cards, so I made enough money in my travels to buy a small farm. Lydia and I lived on our farm about five years, but I was always afraid someone would recognize me."

Cooper said, "So that's why you decided to move to Oregon."

"Yes." Emmett shrugged. "Now out here in the middle of nowhere, after years of not being recognized, this happens."

Cooper asked, "What's the commander going to do?"

"Thank God, he's going to deny I'm the person I'm accused of being. I already relayed all this to him and he's a good man. Of course, those who saw the gunfight may not believe him, but hopefully, I'll be able to lose myself in Oregon like I intended." He suddenly looked tired and turned to Lydia, "Do we need to get Sam?"

"No, he and Tim are with Clarissa."

Emmett stuck his hand out to shake Cooper's. Cooper gripped the small man's hand and marveled that he was shaking the hand of legendary Cheyenne Jack.

Hallie said goodnight to Emmett and hugged Lydia. Touching her elbow, Cooper guided her toward her wagon, several beyond the Hankersons. The clouds shifted and a shaft of moonlight highlighted strands of her hair that had escaped her bonnet. When they reached their campsite, he lifted a finger to push back the strands and she inhaled sharply. He said, "That's quite a story."

She responded with a breathless, "Yes. Yes, it is."

Cooper traced a finger down her cheek, its softness tantalizing his calloused skin. "I wish things could be different." Although he meant his words for Emmett, he knew they were for Hallie.

"Yes," she said again.

When he bent forward, he heard her rapid breathing, and as much as he wanted to crush his mouth over hers, he kissed her cheek. "Goodnight, Hallie."

Chapter 30: Goodbye Farewell Bend; Hello Blue Mountains

Fifty miles northwest of Fort Boise, the train again met up with the Snake River and made its final crossing, now following on the opposite side. When they reached Farewell Bend three days later, it was with mixed emotions. For the last time they viewed the river that had sustained them for over three hundred miles. Although they still had four hundred miles or another month ahead of them, their accomplishments thus far served to energize the travel weary pioneers.

That night, amidst the smoke of dozens of camp fires, friends gathered to relate the tales of their adventures and misadventures, and speculate on the Eden awaiting them at the end of the trail. The Hankersons and several of Mrs. Martinique's gals sat around Hallie's camp fire and watched her render a drawing in the dirt of the perfect layout for a cabin while Tim, with another stick, added his ideas.

Mother and son had obviously overcome their differences and Cooper was happy for them. Tim glanced up and smiled at Cooper. "Mr. Jerome, what do you think of our cabin?"

Cooper squatted beside them. "I like it, but what if the bedroom was moved here?" He pointed with his boot toe and Tim handed him his stick. Before long, they were drawing the barn, cellar, chicken coop, outbuildings, outhouse, and fields, with everyone sharing ideas.

After they could think of nothing more to add to their farm, Hallie sighed and said, "To live in such a place would be heaven on earth."

Unexpectedly, Tim said, "Mr. Jerome, maybe you'll want to move to Oregon after you see our place."

"Appreciate the offer," Cooper replied, "but I have my own place. It's still in the makings of becoming livable, and someday I'll be right proud of it."

Soon, their visitors bid them goodnight and Hallie said, "Son, you'd best head off to bed. Captain Jones said the next few days will be strenuous passing through Burnt River Canyon."

Tim nodded. "Goodnight, Ma. Goodnight, Mr. Jerome."

After he left, Cooper looked at Hallie. "He's a boy to be proud of."

"Thank you," she replied, barely meeting his gaze.

As always, awareness of each other crackled the air. Cooper excused himself to check their readiness for the next day.

The trek through the canyon proved to be some of the roughest of their entire journey. One of their oxen, weakened to the point that Cooper had tied it to the back of the wagon to relieve the poor beast, finally fell to the ground. Sadness enveloped Cooper's heart that the animal had come so far only to die short of a land overflowing with good grazing and plentiful water. With a final pat on the ox's head, he said, "Thank you, old girl, for bringing us this far," and pulled the trigger of his revolver.

It wasn't long after losing their ox that a mule and another ox belonging to other emigrants succumbed to over fifteen hundred miles of travel and their current harsh conditions.

Finally, on the sixth day after entering the canyon, the train made it through and everyone breathed a communal sigh of relief. Traveling treeless land once again, Cooper longed for the shade and comfort of towering oaks and stately pines; even some straggly saplings would be nice.

Captain Jones trotted his horse beside Hallie's wagon and said, "Remember The Lone Tree I told you about before?"

Hallie said, "Yes."

He pointed in the distance. "Well, over there used to be The Lone Pine. I hadn't reached my twentieth birthday the first time I saw it and I remember it being a fine tree. Course, some mindless yokel hacked it down."

Following another train of thought, the captain pointed northeast. "Those are the Blue Mountains." He pointed west. "And those are the Wallowa Mountains. Before we reach the Blue Mountains, we're gonna go through the Grande Ronde Valley and I suspect some of our train will decide to call it home. It's as pretty as a picture."

When the valley was reached, Captain Jones was right; some of their folks decided to stay, among them, the Livermans.

Camped outside a town aptly named LaGrande—having grown along with the emigrants who continued to settle there—the pioneers held a farewell party for those choosing to remain in such a grand location. As the gathering dispersed, Cooper shook Mr. Liverman's hand. "I wish you all the best, Hank." Cooper and Mr.

Liverman had started out with animosity at the Wakarusa River crossing, but ended up fast friends.

"And I wish the same for you, Cooper." He paused. "Maybe it's none of my business, but you and the Wells woman kinda fit like a hand and glove."

Cooper puffed air and Hank hastened to add. "Like I said, none of my business."

Ten days after leaving LaGrande the train camped at Pioneer Springs and the next day, toward the end of August, began their ascent into the Blue Mountains.

Unable to contain her joy, Hallie walked beside Cooper and exclaimed, "This land is positively the most beautiful I have ever seen—so many pines and berries and so much wild game. I fear we shall gorge ourselves to death before we reach our destination."

Cooper laughed. "Well, it's good we're passing through now before the snows make crossing dangerous."

Hallie pondered his words. "I am so grateful that Thomas chose Captain Jones to lead us."

Cooper could sense Hallie wanted to say something more. "Okay, Hallie, what is it you want to ask me?"

She huffed, "How do you do that? How do you read people so well?"

"I have no idea. Now, what do you want to know?"

"You knew Captain Jones before, didn't you?"

"Yes. I served under his command for a short time."

"Why did you hide that information?"

"I haven't hidden anything. Neither one of us thought it necessary information to divulge."

"But you could have told me."

Cooper glanced at her. "Why would I do that?"

Hallie's hurt expression was exactly the reaction he wanted. The more he alienated her, the more she would come to realize there could never be anything between them.

"I see," she said softly, and stepped back to walk beside Tim.

Although beautiful, the mountains soon became almost impossible to cross and a few wagons broke to the point of being irreparable. Two were salvaged into carts, but three more were dismantled for firewood to be shared among the train. The unfortunate emigrants losing their wagons loaded what supplies they could onto their mules or oxen and several folks, including Hallie, helped by carrying some of the supplies on their own beasts or in their wagons.

Mrs. Pittance, now a champion of the underdog, loudly chastised those who did not offer assistance.

After many days of grueling travel, the train finally reached a major campsite for all westward travelers, Emigrant Springs, and camped there for two days enjoying the crystal clear water.

They descended the mountains down Crawford Hill, and at Captain Jones's instruction, the carts were ordered to descend last to prevent injury in case of a runaway wagon. Stubby volunteered to lead the carts and with Sharon by his side, his appearance was so altered from the slimy man he had been, that Hallie would never have recognized him had she not personally witnessed his transformation.

As they headed out of the Blue Mountains, Hallie marveled at the majesty of Mother Nature. Tim pointed out different mountain peaks. "Captain Jones said that mountain is Mount Hood; that one is Mount Adams; and that one is Mount St. Helens."

For several days, Hallie gloried in the changing colors of fall. If the scenery had been a painting, it would have been the most colorful she had ever seen— red, orange, green, yellow, and every shade in between. In beautiful contrast to the brilliant blue sky and puffy white clouds, the sight was enough to steal one's heart and breath. Everyone seemed affected and long silences became the norm.

The emigrants' retrospection, however, came to an end when they reached a division of the trail at the bottom of the mountains, with one path leading north in the direction of the Washington Territory and the other westward across Oregon's Columbia Plateau.

Chapter 31: Decisions...Again

Mrs. Martinique and her gals decided to end their travels in Pendleton, the first notable town below and west of the Blue Mountains. Gossip was that it abounded in bordellos and saloons.

After a heartfelt talk with Clarissa, even offering to share her wagon and home in the Willamette Valley with her, Hallie realized the young woman was dead set on continuing her profession.

Tearfully, Clarissa bid goodbye. "Hallie, you are the most sincere friend I've ever had and I know you want me to change my ways, but I don't have the inclination to do so." She laughed and whispered, "Except I might consider it if Cooper asked me to marry him."

With tears in her own eyes, Hallie laughed and hugged Clarissa. "I shall never forget you."

Clarissa placed her hands on Hallie's shoulders and held her at arm's length. "He loves you, Hallie, but for whatever reason, he's got ghosts that want to rob him of a happily-ever-after." Clarissa continued with conviction, "But you can change that."

Hallie glanced away from the intensity in her dear friend's eyes. "You're wrong, Clarissa."

Clarissa said, "You'll never know if you don't try."

A noise broke up their conversation and Hallie glanced behind her friend to see all the fancy ladies and Mrs. Martinique coming to say their goodbyes. Soon they were joined by Prudence Pittance and her flock and

Hallie witnessed what she considered a miracle—folks so diverse in their beliefs that animosity would have been a natural byproduct—hugging and accepting one another unconditionally.

Hallie and Prudence cried together as they watched Mrs. Martinique's wagons and ladies depart.

After leaving Pendleton, travel again became grueling. The Columbia Plateau was similar to arid plains already crossed and spirits plummeted when water became scarce. A few pioneers talked of returning to fertile areas passed, but after an "Important Particulars" meeting wherein Captain Jones assured everyone that heaven itself lay ahead, they changed their minds, gritted their teeth, and forged onward.

After three weeks and more river crossings, including the Umatilla, John Day, and finally, the Deschutes, the weary emigrants arrived in a town with the unusual name of The Dalles. Elation was soon replaced with trepidation for continuing on meant either a trip down the mighty Columbia River on rafts or overland travel on the Barlow Road.

Captain Jones called another meeting and laid out the options. "Well, pioneers, the first thing I want to say is that I'm mighty proud of ya'll. You've done what most folks only dream of—traveled over two thousand miles to a new land and new beginnings. You've faced famine, drought, sickness, pestilence, mountain peaks, canyons, deserts, plains, rivers, and things too innumerable to mention. You are all heroes in my book and I'm proud that you allowed me to lead you this far. But now it's decision time, again."

He puffed air out his cheeks. "As you can see, we're up against the Columbia River with canyon walls so high they reach to God. There are rafts specially built to haul you, your wagons, and livestock, but they're expensive—and not always successful." He puffed air again. "Another option is to build your own raft, which some pioneers have done and reached their destinations safe and sound...but I wouldn't recommend it." He scratched his earlobe. "A third option is to make your home here. It's beautiful, game and fish are plentiful, and the area is pretty much civilized."

He grinned, paused for emphasis, and then said, "Or you can continue by land on the Barlow Road. I'll not pull any punches; the road is tough, maybe tougher than any we've crossed so far, and you may end up dumping more supplies. But at the end is Oregon City, otherwise known as The End Of The Trail. The toll price to walk the road is a pittance compared to rafting the river." Captain Jones lifted his hat, ran a hand through his thick gray hair and finished with, "This isn't a group vote. This is a decision that each family must decide for itself. Some of you may choose to raft the river, some may choose to remain here, and some may want to continue on the Barlow Road."

Glancing from face to face, the captain finished with, "For those of you continuing overland, we leave day after the morrow." With those words, their fierce leader tipped his hat, mounted Midnight, and rode out of camp.

Chapter 32: The Barlow Road: Conquer or Be Conquered

Cooper cussed at the rutted, rocky road, no doubt, the inspiration of many and varied profane words. The only thing it was good for was keeping his mind off leaving Hallie and Tim. As much as he'd tried to stay aloof these past months, they'd burned their way into his heart.

Holding the reins of Midnight and walking beside Cooper, Captain Jones said, "We need to keep up a good pace so we reach the White River before nightfall. That-a-way, the pioneers can cross when they're rested in the morning."

"Yes, sir," Cooper acknowledged.

The Captain continued, "We got twenty-five wagons, one cart, and several wagons converted to carts. We left Westport with forty-two wagons and one cart." Captain Jones's expression turned reflective. "Not bad in my estimation…not bad at all."

Cooper cussed at another tree root, followed by a rut that jarred the wagon unmercifully, and said, "I'm proud to have served with you in the war and I'm proud to have traveled on this train with you."

Captain Jones shrugged. "Thanks, Cooper. What are your plans after you get the Wells widow settled?"

Captain Jones asked the very thing Cooper didn't want to face at the moment so he avoided the question by asking one of his own. "Are you returning back east anytime soon?"

"Well, only so far as Pendleton." The captain grinned and winked. "Mrs. Martinique is an intelligent woman with whom I look forward to having many long discussions." They walked a little farther and the captain said, "So, by your question, I guess you're thinkin' of headin' back. You know the snows are comin'."

"I know. But I'm sure there are trappers I can hitch up with who know the mountains like the back of their hand."

"Why don't you just stay until spring?"

Cooper frowned. "Not a good idea."

Captain Jones laughed. "Not a good idea for a man fightin' his feelins' for a certain widow woman and her boy, you mean?"

"Not a good idea for a man who's a failure at relationships and living with his own demons."

"I always heard that love conquers everything. Maybe you should give it a try."

"And if it doesn't?"

Captain Jones shrugged. "Then you got a problem."

The train reached the banks of the White River as planned and after much discussion, the leaders decided on the particulars of the following morning's crossing. The crossing proved difficult; two wagons were so badly damaged that the rest of the day was spent converting them into carts also. They couldn't continue on until the next day.

* * *

The pioneers faced the final obstacle in their journey to reach Oregon City and the Willamette Valley—descent down Laurel Hill. Hallie looked to see

Cooper's reaction. Lines at the corners of his mouth and eyes indicated he was not having a good one.

She asked, "How will we get to the bottom? It's so steep."

Cooper pointed to nearby pines. "See those marks? They're scars from ropes. We'll lash the wagons to the trees and slowly let them down."

Hallie's brows arched, concerned. The last time they lowered wagons, a man and four mules died. Whereas the former crevasse allowed wagons to be pulled partially downhill by animals, this one did not. When Hallie's courage began to fail, she forced herself once again to envision the ultimate end—a beautiful cabin and fertile fields in the Willamette Valley.

After a camp meeting with Captain Jones, it was decided that some of the animals and enough men would descend to move carts and wagons out of the way at the bottom, with the carts lowered first. Stubby again volunteered to lead the way. With much trepidation, Hallie watched his cart slowly being let down, praying the entire time. After a scare at about fifty feet, the cart was righted and made it the rest of the way without incident. The men adjusted their maneuvers to compensate for the quick drop at fifty feet and then successfully lowered the rest of the carts. Next, it was time for a wagon and the smallest one was chosen. It, too, was lowered without trouble.

One by one, the wagons reached the bottom of Laurel Hill. Four of the Pittance group's wagons made it safely and then it was time for Prudence's own wagon. All went smoothly, until one of the men yelled, "The rope's about to snap!" As soon as he shouted the words, the threads pulled apart. Their attempt to hold the wagon with the rope lashed to the second tree proved to be too much weight and it also snapped.

Amidst shrieks of horror, the schooner tumbled end-over-end to the bottom and shattered apart.

Whereas most of the emigrants—their faces reflecting the horror of the moment—shrieked or cried, Mrs. Pittance merely glanced at Hallie, shrugged, and said, "A minor inconvenience." Then she smiled.

Hallie gaped at Prudence. The woman had done a complete transformation from the mean-spirited person first encountered over four months previous.

Hallie's wagon, being one of the largest, was lowered last with extra caution, reaching the bottom without mishap.

After that, the pioneers began driving their animals forward and the sure-footed beasts reached the bottom safely. The emigrants, now "mountain men" in their own right, having traversed plains, mountains, canyons, and rivers, began their descent. Men with babies or toddlers strapped to their backs, women holding the hands of their children, teenagers helping the elderly, everyone helping his neighbor, made it to the base of the hill without incident.

When Mrs. Pittance, the last person to step from Laurel Hill, lifted her hands in victory toward the heavens, a shout arose from the weary, rag-tag travelers. Only a few more miles and they would reach Oregon City.

Chapter 33: Beginning Again at the End

Hallie stood with Prudence gazing at Willamette Falls outside of Oregon City. Prudence sighed and said, "We've come a long way, my young friend."

Hallie glimpsed sideways at her, having the feeling Prudence was speaking of more than just physical travel. She agreed, "We certainly have."

Prudence asked, "So, what are your plans?"

"After I locate my land, I'm going to hire men to build a small one-room cabin to winter in. Come next spring I'll plow and plant and hopefully enlarge my cabin. What about you?"

"I've been giving that great consideration. I believe I shall turn my flock over to one of the local pastors—after I know his heart, of course."

Hallie turned a startled gaze on Prudence. "But then, what will you do? You know, you have the fortitude to withstand criticism to become a female leader of her own flock."

Prudence laughed. "That I do. But I have another dream." Lifting her eyes heavenward, she said, "I want to honor my daughters and my husband by founding an orphanage. I want…" her voice broke. "I want children and it doesn't matter if I birthed 'em or not."

Tears filled Hallie's eyes. "And you will be a wonderful mother."

After several minutes of wiping tears and viewing the valley they had given up everything to find, Prudence asked, "What about Cooper?"

Hallie swallowed the lump in her throat. "He's staying until my cabin is built and then returning to Missouri with trappers. I've tried to talk him into staying until spring..." her voice broke, "but he refuses."

Prudence placed an arm around Hallie's shoulders, offering comfort.

* * *

Cooper rode Sweet Pea a short distance from Hallie's log home. Dismounting, he sat on a fallen pine. Her land proved to be exceptional and hiring men to dig a well and erect a cabin and outbuilding suitable for wintering in had not been difficult. Her home, complete with cast iron stove, two windows, and an indoor hand-pump, already had the "woman's touch" he'd encountered when first visiting her in Missouri.

Cooper, who never cried, found himself swallowing back tears. He had accomplished what he'd been hired to do and now it was time to bid Hallie and Tim farewell.

* * *

Hallie tossed restlessly. Cooper was leaving. He hadn't said anything, but she knew with a sixth sense that it was so. Slipping from her bed, she threw on her cape and slippers and quietly left her cabin. A light still burned in the shed. Before her courage failed she knocked lightly on the door.

Cooper opened the door and without a word, stepped aside.

Hallie walked into the tiny room and asked, "You're leaving soon, aren't you?"

"Tomorrow."

She bit her bottom lip to stop its quiver. "You don't have to go. There's land still available. You could farm here. You could use the money you earned bringing me here to buy another farm. Any money you're short, I would gladly give you. You could–"

Cooper placed a finger against her lips. "It's not going to happen, Hallie. I can't stay." His mouth creased in a little smile. "And I can't accept any payment from you…so don't fight me on it. It's my way of atoning for wrongs I have committed. It's what I want."

"But you *can* stay!" she cried, tears streaking her cheeks.

With exquisite tenderness, Cooper wrapped his arms around her and pulled her against his heart.

Hallie said, "I love you, Cooper. I would make you a good wife."

Cooper stroked her hair and whispered against her ear. "I know, sweetheart. But I would not make a good husband."

"You're wrong. You would make me very happy." Turning her mouth until it touched his, she kissed him with so much love she thought she might die from it, and he returned her kiss with the same love. "Let me stay with you all night, Cooper. I have dreamed of being with you. I tried not to, but like Clarissa said, the heart has its own will. If you won't stay, at least let me remember you in lovemaking."

Placing his hands on either side of Hallie's cheeks, Cooper tilted her face so he could gaze directly into her eyes. "Hallie, I want you more than you'll ever know, but I'll not take the chance of leaving you with my child."

"My heart's desire is to bear your child."

In the lamplight, Cooper smiled sadly and stepped away from her. "Goodnight, Hallie." He walked to the door and opened it.

Chapter 34: Sowing and Reaping

For Hallie, the long winter passed slowly and with many tears as she lay in bed every night remembering Cooper. Again and again, she relived special moments during their long journey. No longer did she feel that she was being disloyal to Thomas by loving another man. In fact, she knew Thomas would want her to love such an admirable and compassionate man as Cooper.

When spring finally arrived, she found upstanding men to hire in the preparation and sowing of her fields with the help of her new pastor and fellow worshippers. At first, her neighbors and the establishments where she purchased supplies expressed concern and doubt that a woman could handle the running of a farm. But—like she had assured Cooper—she knew how to farm. Soon, neighbors, both men and women, began asking her advice about their own farm layouts and planting practices.

Summer came and went and her corn and vegetable crops flourished. She became the topic of local conversation with her bumper harvests. Careful budgeting of her funds allowed for the addition of a bedroom to her cabin and a real barn, also a donation to her church, and more importantly, a substantial donation to the Pittance Orphanage, whose building had been donated by a local banker after he had been approached numerous times by a very persistent Prudence Pittance. The orphanage was now the loving home for twenty children, most of whom had lost their parents on the Oregon Trail.

On a beautiful fall day, as Hallie walked toward the orphanage, Stubby and Sharon called to her from the boardwalk. Pleasantly surprised to see them, she said teasingly, "Hello Mr. and Mrs. Newman."

Sharon said, "Hallie, hello! I heard you got a miracle of a crop this year."

"I don't know about it being a miracle, what with it being grown in this fertile valley, but I am pleased with it."

"Well, Stubby and me, we just got hired by Mrs. Pittance to work at the orphanage. It comes with our own room. Stubby's gonna do all the repairs on the building and I'm gonna help with the cooking and cleaning. We've been working odd jobs since we got here, but now that we got something steady we can save for our own place."

Stubby turned from gazing fondly at his wife and said proudly, "I ain't had a drink in over a year now."

Sharon leaned over and kissed her husband's cheek. "And I ain't been with no other man 'ceptin' Stubby."

Hallie smiled at their honesty. "Why don't you come to supper this Sunday?"

Sharon glanced at Stubby, who nodded. "We'd be more'n happy to do that."

Hallie watched the couple continue down the boardwalk and mused that Stubby, someone she had once despised, was now her friend.

Chapter 35: Letter

Cooper walked to the post office next to Jebson's General Store. Rarely did he receive mail and if he did, it was usually from Captain Jones or an army buddy. When he was handed a letter postmarked from Oregon City, Oregon, his heart hammered.

Stepping quickly outside, he carefully opened the envelope.

Dear Mister Jerome,

I'm writin to let ya no how me an ma is doin. We're doin ok. That is I guess we're doin ok. Ma trys not to let me see but she crys lots. She sure misses you. I miss you to. Maybe you mite come see us. Maybe if you talked bout what bothers you it'd make you feel bettr. If you want we could be a real famly. I'd not be mad if you wanted to marry my ma. The way I see it we already missed out on a year we coulda been havin fun. Maybe you'll think bout it?

Tim

Cooper reread the letter several times before returning to Sweet Pea. Mounting and galloping back to his ranch, he knew what he must do.

Within a month, he had harvested his crop, sold his animals and belongings, boarded his cabin up yet again, and packed his mule with necessities. Then he tied the lead of the mule to his saddle, mounted Sweet Pea, and headed out. However, instead of riding west, he rode south.

Chapter 36: Not Just Another Day

On a warm day, late in October, Hallie twisted the lid on the jar of apple jam that Lydia had brought the day before when visiting with Emmett and Sam. Spreading her freshly baked bread with a healthy dose of the treat, she jumped when Tim yelled, "Ma! Ma!" She rushed to the door.

Thrusting the door open, she saw him running toward a man on horseback. Hallie's heart skipped a beat and then hammered like a runaway train. *Cooper!*

She found herself racing across the yard but forced herself to stop and gather her wits. By now, Tim had reached Sweet Pea, and Cooper scooped him up and onto the back of his saddle.

Hallie blinked rapidly to keep her tears in check. *I will not cry. Cooper's seen me crying too many times. I am now a successful farm woman with beautiful land and maybe he's just passing through. Maybe he led another family to Oregon and he's on his return to Missouri.* Hallie kept up a running conversation in her mind as Cooper trotted Sweet Pea forward. *But maybe he's come back because of me.*

About ten feet out, he reined his horse in and lowered Tim down with one arm.

Tim yelled, "Cooper's back!" Then he looked embarrassed. "Ah, I guess you can see that."

Breathlessly, Hallie said, "Hello, Cooper."

"Hello, Hallie." He dismounted.

While Tim kicked dirt clods, Cooper and Hallie stared at each other. Garnering her courage, Hallie finally asked, "Have you come to stay?"

"That I have."

Her eyes widened.

His blue gaze never left her face. "If you'll have me."

"Do you mean like husband and wife?"

"That I do. Will you have me?"

Hallie glanced at Tim to see his reaction. He stood with his foot poised above a clod and one of the widest grins she had ever seen. Tim's joy spurred her into action. With a shout of, "Yes! I'll have you!" she ran and launched herself into Cooper's arms.

Cooper placed his lips against her ear and breathed, "Hallie, my love, I have spent the most miserable year of my life away from you. Will you give me one of your audacious kiss–"

Before he'd finished his sentence, her lips were molded to his in a most audacious kiss.

Tim kicked his dirt clod and shouted, "This is the best day ever!"

Epilogue

Holding Maddie, their three-month-old, Hallie stood beside Cooper waiting for the train to come to a complete stop.

"Would you like me to hold her?" he asked.

Hallie noted his nervousness. "No, honey, you just watch for Jake."

Tim said, "Okay, Pa, you watch that end of the train and I'll watch this end. I seen his picture so I think I'll recognize him."

Cooper smiled. "Thanks, son."

As passengers began alighting, Hallie inhaled deeply to steady her own nervousness. Since his return, Cooper had corresponded diligently with his boy. *No, not a boy. He's a young man.* And now she was about to meet Cooper's eighteen-year-old son for the first time.

Tim pointed and shouted, "I think that's him!"

Both Hallie and Cooper looked anxiously in the direction he indicated. A smile lit Cooper's face and he rushed forward, pausing in front of his son before offering his hand in a shake. Then, with their hands clasped, Cooper pulled his boy into a hug and without hesitation, Jake hugged him back.

Cooper placed his arm around his son's shoulders and guided him toward Hallie and Tim, tears glimmering in his eyes. Hallie swallowed the lump in her throat. How she loved her kind and noble husband. Pride still welled in her heart knowing he had chanced heartbreak by traveling to Texas to seek reconciliation with his boy before returning to Oregon.

As they approached, Hallie got a good look at the young man and marveled at how much he resembled his father, with the same piercing blue eyes and tall frame. Although not as muscular, she had a feeling that within a few years he would be as powerful as Cooper.

Cooper said, "Son, I'd like you to meet my wife, Hallie."

"Howdy ma'am." The boy's Texas twang was endearing.

Cooper lifted the blanket to reveal their baby's face. "And this is your sister, Maddie."

Jake said, "She's so tiny."

Hallie laughed. "But she has a big voice. Just you wait."

Beside Hallie, Tim stood silent. Cooper reached his arm to pull Tim against his other side. "And this is your brother, Tim."

Jake said, "I always wanted a brother or sister and now I have both." He stuck out his hand. "Pleased to meet ya."

Tim grasped his big brother's hand and by the smiles on both their faces, Hallie knew they would forge a deep bond of friendship.

Cooper squeezed the shoulders of his boys and when he turned his beautiful eyes on Hallie's, she knew he had finally lain to rest the ghosts from his past.

With a heartwarming smile, he said, "Let's go home, family."

Research Materials for *Hallie: Cry of the West*

Books:

Portraits of the Riverboats by William C. Davis. Publisher: Thunder Bay Press (hardbound)

Traveling the Oregon Trail, A Falcon Guide, Second Edition by Julie Fanselow. Publisher: Morris Book Publishing, LLC (paperback)

Ox-Team Days on the Oregon Trail by Ezra Meeker in collaboration with Howard R. Driggs, Illustrated by F. N. Wilson. Publisher: World Book Company (ebook)

The Oregon Trail by Michael J. Trinklein. Self Published (ebook)

The Oregon Trail: Sketches of Prairie and Rocky-Mountain Life by Francis Parkman. Public Domain Work (ebook)

Websites:

Books.google.com (*Images of America: Kansas City's Historic Hyde Park* by Patrick Alley and Dona Boley for the Hyde Park Neighborhood Association)

Colecohistsoc.org

Columbiariverimages.com

Essortment.com

Eudorahistory.com

Examiner.net

Faithmemories.com

Freepages.genealogy.rootsweb.ancestry.com

Frontiertrails.com

Hillsboro.k12.mo.us

Historicoregoncity.org

Lonehand.com

OCTA-trails.org

Oregonpioneers.com

Oregontrailcenter.org

PBS.org

Santafetrailresearch.com

Steamboats.com (A special thank you to Nori Muster for replying to my inquiry email)

Thefreedictionary.com

Westporthistorical.com

Wikipedia.com

Youtube.com/watch?v=H616a6LcCxQ (*Landmarks of the Old Oregon Country Episode 6, Part 1* / harold3w)

Author's Note

This has been quite a journey for me. I laughed and wept with the pioneers embarking on the adventure of a lifetime beginning in Missouri and ending in Oregon. I'm certainly relieved that Hallie and Tim made it to the Willamette Valley to begin their new lives and although it took awhile, Cooper eventually worked through his issues to discover the happily-ever-after he so much deserved. Of course, I'm always saddened to leave characters who have become my friends over months of writing, so...to prolong the parting, I often create a series of books. That way, I can revisit the characters from story to story.

As for the next book in the *Finding Home Series,* I have entitled it *Lilah: Rescue on the Rio.* Lilah is Hallie's younger sister who has been on my mind a lot. After leaving home at the age of eighteen, the life she envisioned for herself never came to fruition. In fact, most people would accuse her of living an immoral life, what with being a wealthy man's mistress.

Although the years have been kind to her beauty, she is saddened by what she believes to be a pointless existence and longs to see her sister. However, shame keeps her from traveling the rails that now make the journey to Oregon more easily accomplished.

It has been over twelve years since Hallie moved to Oregon, and although Lilah still receives regular letters from her, she has not responded for over a year.

The fact that Lilah is now thirty-eight and will never have children of her own causes her much melancholia. And it is while she is in this state of mind that Rush Garrett shows up.

Hired by his old army buddy, Cooper Jerome, to find Cooper's sister-in-law, Rush has been a bounty hunter, scout, and trail blazer for twenty years.

In writing the romance of Lilah and Rush, I am attempting to create lonely characters that discover a love beyond anything they could have imagined. I also want to create a feisty woman, a chivalrous albeit no-nonsense cowboy, and lots of adventure that also includes some history of the Old West.

Keep reading for an excerpt from book two in the *Finding Home Series: Rescue on the Rio: Lilah.*

Rescue on the Rio: Lilah (Finding Home Series)

Chapter One: Finding Lilah

June, 1878

Rush Garrett lifted his hand to knock on the elaborate door of the townhouse in a quiet community off the beaten path.

Of course it's on the outskirts; the woman is a rich man's mistress.

The door was opened by a large boned, harsh-faced, housekeeper wearing a white apron. Standing almost as tall as Rush's six-foot-two, she said, "May I help you?"

Rush removed his Stetson. "Yes, ma'am, I'm here to see Miss Lilah Parker."

The housekeeper stared at Rush with such animosity that he was taken aback. Before he could introduce himself, she said curtly, "Follow me," and started walking down the central hallway. She pointed at a hat rack. "You can stow your hat there." Rush did as requested and then followed the stiff-backed woman. His expectation was that he would be ushered into the library or sitting room, but she continued up a staircase at the rear. Following an upstairs hallway leading back toward the front of the house, she paused at a door and knocked three times before opening it.

"Please go in, sir," she said with evident hostility.

Rush lifted an eyebrow, nodded, and stepped past her into a bedroom. The housekeeper quietly shut the door.

Immediately, Rush's attention was drawn to a woman gazing out one of three tall windows overlooking the street. From behind, he admired her upswept honey colored hair with corkscrew curls teasing her graceful neck and bared shoulders. Her lavender dress hugged generous curves and he found himself comparing her to her tiny sister, Hallie. He almost laughed aloud. Whereas his friend's wife was thin and reed like, this woman, at least from behind, was luscious. She turned and Rush's breath whooshed from his chest. Lilah Parker was exotically beautiful with the body of a goddess; a well-endowed goddess.

For a second she seemed unnerved, but composed herself and stepped forward. "Welcome, sir. Please make yourself comfortable. Can I pour you a glass of wine, champagne, or something stronger?"

Rush wanted a shot of whiskey, but he said, "Ah, no ma'am. Thank you, though." He stepped further into the room. The bed to his left was distracting and he wiped images from his mind. This was Hallie's sister and Cooper had hired him to find her and persuade her to come to Oregon for a visit.

The beauty stepped closer and Rush's brain felt like mush. He was just about to introduce himself when she stopped only a hairsbreadth from him. The top of her head reached the middle of his chest. She glanced upward. Now he had a close up of this stunning woman. He knew she was well into her thirties, and although her face was enhanced by women's paints, tiny lines could be seen at the corners of her eyes. Even so, to him, the lines only made her more desirable. Hers was the face of a woman who was anything but simpering. And although she lived in a lovely home, she did not give the impression of being spoiled. She seemed sure of herself, a woman who could hold her own in the world. Oddly, that fact increased her sensuality. However, he never mixed business with pleasure and he needed to reveal the reason for his presence.

Unexpectedly, she reached a hand to the stubble on his face and he stared into gray-green eyes so pale as to seem otherworldly. His gaze roamed her aristocratic bone structure and straight, thin nose. On this woman, a cute up-tilted nose would have been an atrocity.

Her hand moved from his face to the top button of his shirt, and was joined by her other hand. She said, "Would you like me to undress you?"

"Excuse me, ma'am?"

She sighed and her sweet breath distracted him. With nimble fingers, she unbuttoned his top button and moved to the next one. Although he still wore his duster, it did not detract her intent to undress him. Mesmerized, Rush lowered his lids to stare at her pink lips. When the top half of his shirt was unbuttoned, she slid her hands inside and caressed his upper body. For a second, he closed his eyes and wanted to give in to the craziness of the moment, but loyalty to his friends, as well as his gentlemanly instincts, would not allow it.

Lifting his hands, he grasped her wrists to still her movements. "Ma'am, I think you've confused me with someone else. My name is Rush Garrett and I've been hired by your brother-in-law, Cooper Jerome, and your sister, Hallie, to find you and bring you to Oregon."

The courtesan's eyes widened and she jerked her hands from inside his shirt at the same time she jumped backwards. Her foot caught on a throw rug and she started to topple. Rush grabbed her by the waist and jerked her forward, which brought her body flush against his, and he almost groaned as the lushness of her breasts molded to his lower chest. Lifting her hands, she pushed against him and backed away again.

Her voice sounded breathless and her lips trembled when she said, "I-I don't understand."

Patiently, Rush buttoned his shirt, and said, "I'm a friend of your brother-in-law. We served together as Northerners in the war, and, well, I'm sort of in the business of finding people, so he hired me to locate you." He reached into the pocket of his duster and retrieved an envelope. "This letter from your sister will explain everything." He stepped forward and the woman stepped backwards. Rather than approach her, he laid the letter on a nearby table.

"Ma'am, I'll just wait downstairs while you read it."

Novels and Novellas by Verna Clay

CONTEMPORARY ROMANCE

<u>Western</u>

Romance on the Ranch Series
Dream Kisses
Honey Kisses
Baby Kisses
Candy Kisses
Christmas Kisses
Rock Star Kisses
Forever Kisses
Forgotten Kisses
Angel Kisses
The Last Kiss

Oasis, Arizona Series
Stranded in Oasis
Branded in Oasis
Crashed in Oasis

<u>Paranormal</u>

Finding SOMEWHERE Series
SOMEWHERE by the Sea
SOMEWHERE to Spend Christmas
SOMEWHERE for a Hero to Hide
SOMEWHERE to Begin Again
SOMEWHERE to Fall in Love

HISTORICAL ROMANCE

Unconventional Series
*Abby: Mail Order Bride
Broken Angel
Ryder's Salvation
Joy's Return

*2014 Gold Medal Winner Readers' Favorite Int'l Book Contest

Historical Romance

Finding Home Series
Cry of the West: Hallie
Rescue on the Rio: Lilah
Missouri Challenge: Daisy

Red Rocks Trilogy: Past Present Future
Healing Woman of the Red Rocks (Past)
Song of the Red Rocks (Present)
Spirit Tree of the Red Rocks (Future)

Journeys of the Heart Novellas
Violet's Vindication
Priscilla's Pride
Samuel's Sacrifice

FANTASY ROMANCE

Shapeling Trilogy
Roth: Protector (Book 1)
Fawn: Master (Book 2)
Davide: Prince (Book 3)

Jazmine

YOUNG ADULT ROMANCE
(Verna Clay writing as Colleen Clay)

Fragile Hearts

AUDIO BOOKS

Abby: Mail Order Bride
Broken Angel
Cry of the West: Hallie
Dream Kisses
Honey Kisses
Baby Kisses
SOMEWHERE by the Sea
SOMEWHERE to Spend Christmas
SOMEWHERE for a Hero to Hide

LARGE PRINT PAPERBACKS

SOMEWHERE by the Sea
SOMEWHERE to Spend Christmas
SOMEWHERE for a Hero to Hide
SOMEWHERE to Begin Again
SOMEWHERE to Fall in Love

Made in the USA
Monee, IL
10 July 2021

73324316R00156